With thanks to Richard,
who supported me in all of this.

For my friend whose life compelled me to
imagine and write this story.

For dear friends who read, commented on
and corrected my writing.

Above all, to God whose mercy, grace and
wisdom "cannot be valued with the gold of
Ophir, with the precious onyx, or the
sapphire".

1

HOT. STUFFY. SUFFOCATING. MARTHA TRIES TO lower her face deeper into the pillow to escape the pressure on her face. Sweat trickles down her back, her hands clench the bedsheets. Pushing her forehead down, she moves her face side to side as much as possible, fighting for air. She struggles on, desperately pushing down to get away from the weight. It doesn't work. Her breath sounds loud, rasping in her ears, mixing with her heartbeat. Panic is making her breath shallow, black and red specks clouding her vision.

Just when she thinks that she will have to give in to the stealthily advancing darkness, another sound mixes in. A sharp, chirping sound, so out of place that all others sounds stop. Her heartbeat quietens down, the rushing, pulsating noise stops, and there is only the new sound. Her next breath is a large gulping one, deep and cleansing. Martha stares ahead blankly, realising she is now staring at the wall, rather than trying to use her nose like a drill to bore through her bedding and mattress, digging desperately for air! Her face is no longer being pushed into the pillow, there is no vice-like hand on the back of her neck anymore. In fact, she is half sitting up, her ears having followed the weird chirping sound. She breathes in and out a few times, as if to convince herself that oxygen is now in free supply once more.

"It was a dream," she whispers, still hardly able to believe it was just that. "I'm not being held down, not this time..." She can feel the shakes starting now, always at the same place in her body, always in her shoulders first, causing them to cramp together, going more and more rigid, with her arms seizing up, then the rest of her body shaking and convulsing. "Breathe... Just breathe. I'm not a victim, I'm a victor." The way her voice shakes and squeaks totally undoes the message. "I can do all things through Christ who strengthens me," she continues, concentrating on breathing in... and out... counting, concentrating, whispering the words through lips that feel frozen. But Martha keeps going, her fingers clenching and unclenching along with her deep breathing. It works, as it always does, eventually. Her breathing becomes more normal as her shoulders relax, and after a while she knows she is back. Back to reality, back to here and now, back to safety.

She leans into the pillows, free to take in her surroundings. The room is called a studio, she remembers, looking at the little light where the cooker is connected to the wall. The studio is very hot, very stuffy, and she sighs. "I should have guessed." She wipes her wet forehead, the sweat cooling her down, causing her to shiver, but not as convulsively as earlier. "I should have..." Yes, that was the problem, she realises. Outside it had still been very warm when she went to bed, after locking the door carefully, checking all the windows were tightly shut, rechecking the door. She had looked at the air conditioning unit on the wall, but decided it was too expensive. "I will be fine," she remembers mumbling. *Well, talk about famous last words...!* She sighs, rubbing her arms to warm herself up a little, then pads over to the window, and opens it a little. The chirping sound is suddenly a lot louder, and Martha smiles. "Thanks, cicada, for pulling me out of my nightmare! Your sound is so unusual, it actually got through to me!" She feels grateful to whichever little cicada it was, and shudders when she remembers the nightmare. Flashback, more accurately, but Martha prefers to call it a nightmare, just to tell herself that it's not real. At least, not real anymore!

She leans out of the large window, looking into the still warm night air. She can see the first light glittering on the water, outlining the mountains at the back of the resort. She sniffs in the air that is so different from the hearty Cotswold air. "Just what the doctor ordered," she says, ignoring the little shiver deep inside when she looks at all things new. "I can do all things," she repeats, her voice a lot more convincing now, her hands clenching the windowsill in determination. "A new day, well, *almost* day at least, and a new chapter." She spots her journal and smiles, her face transformed by the unusual expression. Martha stands motionless, surprised by her sudden feeling of... can it be joy? She turns away from the window, picks up her journal, and sits down at the small dining table. She opens the new, fresh pages, loving the feeling of brand-new notebooks, and this one is definitely a very beautiful one. Her pen hovers over the first page, wondering how to put into words what she just felt.

"September the second. Woke up in a panic, cicadas got me out of the attack, looked out of the window, thought of this new venture, and felt happy." *That does sound a little pathetic, but then, my life is a bit pathetic,* she thinks.

"I need more sleep, all this thinking about happiness and joy, well, things are never what they look like anyway, and I don't even know why I'm up at this time. I'll regret it in the morning, no doubt." Martha pulls a face, feeling her heartbeat speeding up over this diversion, almost rushing back to bed. Once lying down, she spots the open window and hesitates. Should she close it? "I really don't want to get too hot again," she groans, "and also, there is a sheer drop, so be sensible," hoping that her stern words will be believed by her head.

She can feel the unease over having written in the morning, her sudden note in the new journal. "I always write in the evening; I don't know why I just did that!" Looking at the window, still a little bothered by the fact it's open, Martha suddenly remembers that smile. "Maybe it's a good thing I wrote it down." She realises all too well that when the morning comes, that fleeting feeling might well be long forgotten, and she turns on her side, feeling pleased that at least it's now in her journal, black on white.

Her alarm wakes her up a few hours later, and as always, Martha feels her heart racing, her body automatically moving to the edge of the bed. Like all mornings, she forces herself to hit the snooze button, her hand shaking a little bit at this act of rebellion. She snuggles back down. "Done it! Again! These ten minutes are mine." She forces her breathing to slow down and makes her muscles go soft, pretending to herself that she is having a relaxing lie in, wondering if this will ever become her new normal. She can still hear William's posh voice shouting at her, telling her to get a move on, and whether her ears need sorting out too... She shivers, closes her eyes and whispers, "I'm not a victim, I'm a victor. The past has passed." When the alarm goes again, she gets up and walks to the bathroom where her clothes have been put ready, relieved that the ten minutes of waiting have gone. By the time Martha is ready to go down for breakfast she is feeling a little better. Following her morning routine has made the start of the day feel more normal, although she knows full well that there will be nothing routine about this day!

Martha finds the dining room without trouble and chooses a corner table. She puts the tray down, looking round warily. She makes sure her back is against the wall and stirs her black tea whilst looking round the large dining room. It's beautifully done, with huge windows letting in the morning sun. Beyond the outside terrace she can see the large pool area and then the beach. Martha feels the thrill, the beauty of the place soothing her, calming her. Looking round at the other guests, she knows that she will need all the calm she can find! "That beach looks wonderful, and I'm sure I can smell the sea from here," she mumbles, her keenness fading just a little when she spots the many sun umbrellas along the beach. "There must be some quiet spots as well. Maybe certain times of the day there will be no other guests..." Knowing how large the resort is, somehow that feels like vain hope.

She looks round the dining room again. The place is decorated with Cretan art and painted in light colours. Tables are set in alcoves as well as in the open space in the middle. Even though there must be space for many guests, it still remains a place to feel at home and enjoy a meal.

Martha stirs and stirs, her toast untouched, her stomach churning away.

An older woman walks into the dining room, nodding and smiling at various guests, until her eye catches Martha. She comes across to her table straight away and holds out her hand, smiling. "You must be Martha Taylor? Welcome to Sapphire Beach Resort. Do you mind if I join you?" Without waiting for an answer, she walks over to the buffet and soon joins Martha at the little table. "My name is Joan, by the way," the older woman says, "you'll be taking over from me. I was the holiday rep here, but the girl who did the smaller resorts and self-catering had to go home unexpectedly. I have a car here, as I live here all year round, so that's why the job came up."

Martha nods, feeling nervous and awkward, unsure what to say.

"Have you done holiday rep work before?" Joan continues between mouthfuls.

Martha manages to shake her head. "No… um… no, not really. I… um… I had a summer job once in Weston-Super-Mare, so I'm hoping I'll be alright. It just sounded interesting," she says, trying to pull what she hopes will pass for a confident, happy smile, her eyes not joining in.

Joan nods and smiles back, her eyes happy and carefree though, and Martha stirs her tea a bit more. "You'll be fine," Joan says with confidence. "It's September, so most guests have gone home anyway, and the resort is very organised. Did you look through the material about the resort at all?"

Martha nods eagerly. "Yes, yes I did. I enjoyed that too; it seems to offer some lovely things!" She pulls her small, fat notebook out of her bag. The notebook looks well used, and for a second she rests the tips of her fingers on its cover. "I've written it all down in my Lifeline," she says, her quick grimace appearing, "just to make sure I don't forget or overlook anything."

Getting her pen out she carefully writes, "Joan, previous rep, breakfast," in the little book. She hesitates. Does she need to write down that Joan has now taken over the smaller resorts, or is that an unimportant detail? In the end she leaves it, a little bothered by it.

"The view is lovely," Martha says, looking up at Joan, wondering if her comment paints her as a total novice to travelling or not. "Just the colour of the pool, and the beach... So many different types of blue – and the orange umbrellas! The colours together are just lovely, such a nice way to start the day!" She just suddenly felt she wanted to share that with Joan, but she immediately regrets it. "You're probably used to it," she adds. Martha can feel her shoulders tightening up, tension growing in her neck, the hand with the little teaspoon shaking slightly, making the spoon clatter against the sides of her cup.

"Oh, I agree!" Joan gushes. "I see what you mean with all the colours. You're right! You know, I never even noticed! I sit here most mornings, and I do adore the view, but you've really made me realise the combination of different blues," she says. She looks at Martha with pleasure, making Martha feel... odd. Her fingers feel cold, clammy, but again Martha feels her mouth pulling itself into a smile, a real one. She can feel her eyes joining in this time, and again there is that tiny sensation of joy. Her smile stays on when her eyes roam free, thinking that she might have to make another note in her journal this evening: "Joy came knocking on my heart's door again, this time caused by another rep."

Martha finds suddenly that she has eaten the piece of toast as well as finally finished her cold tea.

Joan nods and stands up. "Let me show you around and explain stuff around here."

2

JOAN SHOWS MARTHA ROUND THE RESORT, which is built right on the beach. To the side of the resort is a little stream, splattering over rocks, gushing with enthusiasm to join the sea. The resort is bright and cheerful, the walls of the accommodation a pale yellow. Trees, shrubs and plants make it look lush and welcoming. It's quiet this time of year, and the main noise is from raucous cicadas. Martha's eyes shine, even though she isn't aware of that. Just the richness of the colours, the beautiful artwork on the walls, the huge amphora in one corner…

"What a wonderful place," she sighs to Joan. "Sorry, could you repeat that last bit one more time? I do apologise, it's just… I want to make sure I get the instructions right, you see," she adds, writing furiously in her little notebook.

"After each arrival day I do an overview session in the pool area, or in the dining room if it's wet. No, I agree, that won't happen very often, I'm sure! So I give them all the leaflet about the resort, with my special number on it. I check if they have any questions or specific things they want to see or do. This is the list with options and how to set it up."

Martha glances at the long list with excursions in her hand.

Joan smiles, her kind eyes taking in the slight woman in front of her, nervous hands scribbling away at top speed. Every now and then Martha stops to poke at the bridge of her glasses to push them up higher. The glasses look expensive, the gold frame delicate, and Joan fervently hopes they can stand the rushed jabs aimed at them! *Finding a suitable optician in this part of Crete could be interesting...* "Now, here is the checklist to run through with guests. Just study the list a little before the first ones arrive, alright? Then it doesn't sound like a long tick box exercise," she laughs. "Just make sure they understand. Now, the one that you might have to explain a bit is the toilet paper one. Some people will know, of course, but it's good to explain that all toilet paper must be put in the small bins provided. The system is just not designed to deal with paper. Of course, bins are emptied every day."

Martha nods, putting an extra mark in front of that particular point on the checklist.

"Now, what else do I need to tell you?" Joan looks at the list, humming at each point. "Well, the rest sort of explains itself, really. Ah yes, the excursions. Now, on the second list there are a few more local ones – you know, boat trips, that sort of thing. If it's something you like to do, you are welcome to go along. There is something about that on the back; I made a quick note for you, so I hope you can understand my writing... worse than a doctor, my husband always says. Let's go down to the dining area again for a quick drink and then I'll be off," she suggests, and they go back the way they came, Martha holding the map, the other papers and her Lifeline.

14

Joan drops her bag down, gets a coffee and quickly asks something from one of the holidaymakers sitting at a large table. Martha gets herself another black tea, almost spilling it as a very loud holidaymaker calls out to someone outside on the terrace. She sits down at the small table, opposite Joan's bag, glad that they managed to get the same table as they had at breakfast time. Joan looks at her when she gets back and frowns a little. "Are you alright?" she asks, noting Martha's pale face and slightly shaking hands.

Martha nods. "Yes, thanks. It was just that loud man; I wasn't expecting it," she grins with her extra-large smile, and vigorously stirs her tea to hide her shaking hands. "I'm just not keen on loud noises," she explains hurriedly, as she can see that Joan is looking round to see if she can spot the cause of her nerves. "I lived most of my life in small villages," she adds, knowing that she really needs to stop, as she is making too much of the incident. Martha forces herself to put her teaspoon down, and to even out her breathing. Looking at a large painting of warm orange and royal blue helps her to calm down. "That is such a warm picture," she says, just taking her eyes off the painting long enough to point it out to Joan. "Those colours are just stunning," she sighs happily, the loud holidaymaker forgotten, her list with things to remember as well.

Joan looks round at the painting and wholeheartedly agrees. "On your next day off, you should get the bus to Iraklion," she suggests. "There are a lot of shops there, and you will find some beautiful art books there for reasonable prices. I'll text you some addresses, as you'll want to go along the little back streets, not the main tourist drag; it's busy and expensive. You'll love the museum as well – if you're keen on history?" Joan rummages in her large handbag and pulls out the map of the resort and local small town. "Look, remember I told you about the bus stop? It's right here, and buses go to Iraklion regularly and they only take about half an hour. Now, bus stations in Iraklion are a bit complex; it's in the material I left with you. To get there is very easy though; you'll love it."

Martha feels a little thrill. Go to the main city, and find some beautiful art books about Crete? On the other hand, will she be able to work out how the buses work? She thinks back to her recent months in the Cotswolds, living with her sister and brother-in-law. She just about managed the bus to and from Cheltenham, but even that was too much most days. The trip to the airport with her sister by train had nearly driven her sister to distraction. Martha checked, double-checked and triple-checked that they were definitely on the right train. By the time she got to the airport she was exhausted – the airport itself nearly being her undoing with the noise, movement and number of people pushing past her. It was only her sister's calm presence that got her on the plane alive. She had a great reason that time; after all, she was expected for work. Getting some beautiful artbooks might not be enough reason to go through an ordeal like that. The thought of getting on a foreign bus going to an unknown city makes her tea slosh around her stomach already. What if she gets lost, away from the "tourist drag" with nobody to ask for help? Will they even speak English in the non-touristy area? Joan's idea of easy doesn't make Martha feel any better. "How well do people in Crete speak English?" she asks, "I mean, outside the tourist places?"

Before Joan can answer, a large man appears at their table, his moustache matching his size, with an open-neck shirt and very expensive looking leather sandals. He looks from one rep to the other and his red face doesn't get any happier. "Are you two planning on coffee housing all day?" he asks in the end, glaring at Martha especially. "Did you tell that lady with the poodle where to walk her dog without troubles?" he adds, to Joan now, frowning even harder, looking around their table as if he expects the poodle to appear any moment. "Anyway, look lively!" Away he stomps, leaving Joan to roll her eyes, sipping her coffee peacefully.

Martha gulps, and by breathing faster and deeper manages to force her hands to stir her cooling tea one last time, before lifting the cup in shaking hands. She lifts the cup to her lips, but lowers it quickly, as she doesn't think her hands will cooperate long enough for her to actually drink the tea. She glances at Joan, hardly noticing her, before her eyes dart round looking for the large grump. Who was he? Where did he suddenly come from? How could she have missed him coming in?

Joan's warm, calm hand grips Martha's, giving her a start. "Don't worry about him; he's the manager and he's getting tired, obviously. The season is almost over, he's like this every year. He just likes to throw his weight around," she giggles suddenly, and adds, "and yes, before you ask, the poodle lady is all sorted! No rush about your tea; just take your time, dear." She smiles warmly at Martha and squeezes her hand before she lets go.

Martha nods, hiding her shaking hands under the table, hooking her fingers together as she tries to calm down again.

"Honestly, Martha, he really is alright; you really don't need to worry about him. He's been very good to the reps every year and really takes care of all staff members. Better than most resorts, I must say."

Martha smiles her large grin and somehow manages to drink her tea; then they walk out of the dining room together.

"Come to my car. I have the leaflets in there; it's a box full of them! I hope you'll have a lovely time here; the sea is lovely, so is the little town. Just one warning..." Joan's eyes start to sparkle, and she can hardly contain her loud giggles. "You see, there is a little saying that Sapphire Beach leads to a sapphire ring!"

"Thank you," Martha says, her voice only a little thin, coughing out a laugh, then she spots the ladies' bathroom. "Excuse me a moment," she says, and her deliberate steps last until she is on the other side of the door. Then Martha dashes into the toilet cubicle, glad she only had a little toast and some tea this morning. She wipes her mouth with shaking hands, remembering the little bin, then washes her hands with cold water. The owlish eyes staring back at her in the mirror make her take a deep, shuddering breath. "I'm not a victim, I'm a victor. I can do all things through Christ..." She hesitates. *Well, all things apart from loud holidaymakers and grumpy managers, it seems... or rings!* She pokes her glasses up firmly, tucks her hair behind her left ear in a quick gesture and repeats with determination, "I *can* do all things through Christ who strengthens me!" She nods at herself in the mirror, then joins Joan and walks with her to the car park behind the resort to pick up the leaflets for her clients.

Joan makes sure Martha has her number, and with a last few encouragements, climbs into her tiny car and disappears round the dusty corner. Martha walks slowly back to her studio, trying to remember as much as possible, staring at the map of the resort, her studio marked with a large black circle.

"Good thing I have the rest of the day free, so I can look through all this stuff and set up how I'm going to do things and make a list of what I need to do tomorrow." She can feel excitement growing as well as the weight in her now very empty stomach. "How will I remember all this? What if the manager gets really annoyed with me? What if I'm alone and I meet him in a bad mood...?" She swallows. "I'm a victor, I will be a victor; I can do this, of course I can," and she gives a laugh that doesn't sound amused at all. She shudders, blushes and tries again. After a few practices she is nearly in tears, giving up on laughing in a natural way for now.

Glasses straight, hair tucked behind her ear, Martha pulls her Lifeline from her bag and sits down at her table with the leaflets, maps and instructions. She finds herself looking outside until she can't stand it any longer! With her water bottle and all the necessary papers, she moves to the little balcony overlooking the sea and tiny inlet, the incredible blue water making her blink. The little table outside is soon covered in papers, and Martha sighs, then looks up with a jolt. "I'm smiling again! Thank you, Lord... although..." She stops herself. "Let's not go there. Now, where is the list with instructions? It says in the

Lifeline that I will need to know them, so there must be a paper, I presume…"

Martha also looks through the list with excursions, to make sure she knows what's on offer. It's a long list, with very varied day trips, catering to all kinds of holiday-makers. She is half-tempted for a moment by the descriptions of some trips, but then she reminds herself that she will be stuck with lots of people that she doesn't know and who might be very loud and rude. That would leave her in a panic with all the horrible consequences of that. Of course, not everyone will be like that. Most of them will be nice enough, but their friendliness might make them want to speak to her more than she is comfortable with… She sighs, knowing that she's missing out just because of her fears. She manages to tell herself that she'll need some rest this month and traipsing all over Crete will just leave her exhausted and unable to do her job. She almost manages to convince herself, but her heart feels sad, tugging at her whilst looking at the colourful pictures.

3

LUNCHTIME FINDS THE LITTLE BALCONLY VERY hot, and Martha blows a stray, clingy hair off her face, tucks her hair behind her left ear, prods her glasses back where they belong, and looks at the mountains. They seem to shimmer in the heat, and suddenly she decides that, really, the balcony is too hot to work. She gathers up the papers and notebook, taking them inside, suddenly feeling unsure whether working out on the balcony was actually a good choice. "After all, I was using the table indoors, and it's cooler there. Maybe I should have just stayed there?" She hesitates, trying to tell herself that it really doesn't matter, that any table was fine, that she is in a holiday resort, after all; *it's where people go for the sun, don't they?* She blinks rapidly, trying to put a stop to her pointless thoughts, and puts the papers in a neat pile into the drawer, her notebook in the right pocket of her handbag. She washes her hands, brushes her hair, looks round... "Come on, it's lunchtime; you know it is," she mutters, knowing that she is just buying time. A look at her watch gives her a jolt, making her feel clammy straight away. "It really is lunchtime; you know he hates..." She stops, tears coming into her eyes as she realises that having lunch a few minutes later than she would normally have it is not a problem at all! For a second, she debates whether to delay her lunch on purpose, just for a few more minutes, but decides to go down to the dining room anyway, the idea of being even later unnerving her. "Of course, I could delay lunch if I wanted to; I'm only going because I have decided to do so," she mutters defiantly.

Martha walks into the sunny dining room and stops abruptly. The clamminess returns with a vengeance and she almost turns round to walk out. At the last moment she remembers her position at the resort and all that entails. Her icy fingers grapple for the locket on the golden chain round her neck, and somehow her eyes manage to locate the food table. Her wide-open eyes stare at the table, itching to blink, but she wills them open. She is determined to keep the table in view, and the table only, fearing that if she would blink, the buffet might disappear or she might pass out, either option too dreadful for her to allow it. Taking careful, deliberate steps she walks towards the large buffet, smiling at people that she passes.

"I made it," she breathes when she gets to the buffet. "That's one. Getting the food and some tea is two, and actually making it to a table is three. I can do all things…" The sights and smells of food make her stomach do funny backflips; at least, that is the image she tries to conjure up. Admitting that her stomach is doing its best to have her dash to the bathroom is too… *pathetic* – a posh Voice supplies the word.

"You're utterly pathetic, you do know that, darling?" The Voice managed to make "darling" sound like a bad word. *"I don't know how you get through a day, to be honest. Or how you even have a common day job,"* the Voice hammers on.

22

Martha finds herself shaking, her vision blurring – the Voice is all too real. She is no longer in the large, sun-filled dining room of the resort, but in the expensive, antique-filled dining room that used to be her home. Martha knows it's not real, but has no way of escape, just as she didn't that time. One shaking hand reaches up and clutches her locket.

Suddenly a loud laugh makes her jump. Martha's eyes fly open, blinking against the sunlight that is almost blinding her; its contrast with the dark dining room couldn't be greater. The Voice fades away as well and Martha gasps, finds herself clutching the buffet table. She leans over the food a little, pretending to study the descriptions and feigning great interest in the dishes to hide her tear-filled eyes.

Martha closes her eyes again for a moment; searching, praying for strength – just a little strength, enough to make it through numbers two and three on her list! Breathing in and out, counting slowly in her head, she manages to calm herself sufficiently to lift an empty plate and walk stiffly to the fruit area. She puts some watermelon on her plate and spots the sticky mess called baklava. She finds her face relaxing, and almost smiling. She has only ever seen pictures of baklava, but the description sounded amazing: "sticky, sweet, dripping with honey and nuts..."

"Just the thing I need," she says quietly, memories of the Voice shifting further and further back in her mind. "Now for some tea, and then I'll have made it through number two. I'm a victor, not a victim!" Even though her plate wobbles dangerously, she can feel the shaking decrease with each careful step.

Soon Martha spots a table outside, shaded, at the edge of the terrace. With a sigh of relief, she sinks down in the chair. "And that is three!" she thinks, feeling a proper overcomer. "I made it," she says, sinking her teeth into the sticky layers of pastry. "Ooh, this is good! So sweet – but amazing!" The pastry crunches in a most satisfying manner, and the nuts and honey are the perfect combination. She looks at the baklava, wondering how it's made. Again, there is that unfamiliar pull at the corners of her mouth, and Martha's eyes light up as she finds herself smiling again.

The baklava and watermelon settle her stomach, and Martha manages to look round the dining area without her heartrate increasing. The low-level noise sounds like a murmuring brook in the Cotswolds, making its way over large rocks. It is actually quite soothing, now that she thinks about it. She smiles at a nearby elderly couple, nods at a young woman walking nearby, and leans back in her chair, amazed at the heat even in the shade! The warmth is comfortable though, and makes her feel sleepy, drowsy even.

"So, these are my clients," she thinks, looking around the various tables inside and out on the terrace. "Most people seem very nice; I'm sure they'll be alright," she says to herself, trying to ignore the little panic flags being raised all over her mind. "Should I be somewhere this afternoon? I met the other rep this morning, didn't I? It was this morning, surely?" With trembling hands Martha starts digging in her bag for her Lifeline, all drowsiness gone. The stout notebook on the table, she flicks through the pages. "Yes, Joan. I met her this morning in the dining room. Ah, I remember... We sat inside. Now, let me look at my schedule." Martha tucks her hair behind her ear, the clump of hair feeling a little greasy already, a sign she has been touching it too many times. "It's probably covered in baklava," she sighs, wondering again whether she is actually able to do this job. Then she says, "Of course I can," determined to believe her own words and to put a stop to these doubts. "Lots of people are holiday reps, sometimes very young people, and I'm sure I can do the job of an older teenager!"

The Voice can be heard in the recesses of her mind: "…common day job … impossible to find somebody else, so they made do with you, did they?"

Tears make her glasses steam up a little, so Martha blinks and blinks to clear her eyes of the excess dampness, looking over the pool and beach, naming all the different colours and shades she can see, to drown out the Voice. It works, the soothing motion of the waves with their rustling noise calming her, replacing the ugly words.

"I can do all things," she says. "I know I can, and I will do this job as well as I can." She looks down in the notebook, her finger tracing the days and times. *This afternoon I should be available to answer questions here on the terrace. Well, that's good; this table will be perfect! I wonder how many people will have questions? Hopefully Joan will have listed all the things I will need to know, and I know I made a list too. It will be in my studio, so I will need to bring that here as well. What will the clients be like, I wonder… If it's that older couple, I wouldn't mind,* she thinks, looking at the older couple, the lady wearing a plain cotton dress. *She looks lovely in that dress; the colour suits her. That shirt looks dreadful on her husband, but he is very smiley, with kind eyes.*

Their voices are so quiet, I can't hear them at all! Yes, I hope whoever comes this afternoon will be like them!

Martha looks at the door leading into the inside dining room. When looking for Joan's name she spotted the line about the manager. "Moustache, is tired of the season," she had written down. Funnily enough, she remembers him but struggles to remember what Joan looked like! She finds herself looking round again and realises that all through her meal she subconsciously has kept an eye out for the manager! *Oh dear. I know why I wrote down that he is tired... I need an excuse for his loudness.* Draining the last bit of her cold tea, Martha decides to prepare for her question and (hopefully) answer session.

Martha carefully lists all that she needs for the next three hours, starting with fresh black tea; her Lifeline, of course, then the leaflets of the hotel, her own map of the hotel and area, and her general information folder, which is huge. Impulsively she lists "baklava" on her list and finds herself doing a throaty rattle, which could almost pass for a rough giggle! She stops writing in surprise and feels the now more familiar tug at her lips. She looks out over the sea, *the colour probably best described as Persian blue,* she decides dreamily, *or is it more Egyptian blue?* "Such a beautiful shade," she sighs, an odd feeling coming over her. She forgets all about the job for the moment, forgets about the list, forgets about the clients and the way they worry and intimidate her. *This almost feels like I'm happy, Lord, and that scares me more than anything,* she thinks, but still her eyes stay staring at the lapping waves, crackling and cackling over the sand and shells. Martha just sits there, enthralled, and feeling tiny slithers of peace rolling into her heart with each new wave.

4

MARTHA CAREFULLY ARRANGES HER PAPERS
on the table in front of her. She makes sure her back is
towards the white trellis enclosing the terrace. Her hands
are shaking and twice she almost spills her black tea over
the papers. She sits down, having arranged some chairs on
the other side of the table for whichever clients will turn
up. She sits down, sips her tea, then looks at the papers in
front of her. For one awful moment her mind goes blank.
"What am I doing? What is my job? What do I need to
do?" Her breathing instantly speeds up, she can feel her
shoulders tightening up, her arms start their familiar
shaking. "No, Lord, please, not now!" With immense
effort she lifts her hand; shaking fingers that seem to
belong to somebody else slide over the locket, warm to the
touch. Somehow, the warm gold makes her fingers feel
part of her again. She gasps, and tries to count, not
making it past three each time she tries. Black dots wander
across her vision from left to right, and back again. There
is a crashing, shattering sound, and hot liquid spills over
her bare feet in sandals.

Martha stops, just holding her breath, her fingers tight
round the locket, and in her head counts calmly and
clearly to ten. Then all the way down to zero. The shaking
is reduced to shivers; all her eyes can see is blue sky, blue

swimming pool, blue sea, but different kinds of blue. She has to take her gold-rimmed glasses off, setting them carefully on her table to dry in the warm air. From her bag she gets some tissues to dry her feet after quickly dabbing at her face first. Under the table, she breathes, "Thank you, Lord. Not quite what I had in mind to end that panic attack, but I'll take it..." She pulls a face as well. "Lots of my life hasn't been what I had in mind – it still isn't, and I would rather not have taken it – but it seems I didn't have a choice... or maybe I did... Well..." She stops, not sure that her mind is going along a very wise track there! Martha knows that once her mind is off on this track, it will be hard to stop. The track will get more and more rocky, darker, more painful, and even if she does somehow manage to stop herself, the effect will stay with her. Nothing good will come of this track, only regrets and 'what ifs' and accusations whispered in her heart which she will then feel guilty about. After all, God is sovereign, He has no obligation to help her, has He? He gave her so much, and she knows He gave her choices as well as instructions of how to choose. Somehow, she resented the instructions as well as the choices, feeling overwhelmed by the responsibility. Martha just wanted to live her life, a good life, without having to choose wisely, but she wanted the right doors to be automatic doors, not revolving doors, spinning her till she didn't remember which way was straight ahead. Martha looks around the sunny terrace, still feeling like she is trapped in a dark place without doors, without lights or windows, and it takes all of her courage to mutter to herself that even if there is no way, God will make a way, a good way, a straight but narrow way, a way leading to life. She sighs, wishing that she could truly believe and trust this, truly feel free to open doors.

She finds a waitress happy to help her clear up the remains of her mug, and is grateful for a fresh mug of black tea. To fill the time until a client appears, she flicks through her huge folder with information again. Some of the photographs look stunning! "The rocks in that gorge... It would make an amazing charcoal drawing; the sharp lines here, the smoother ones that side..." Her thin fingers trace the picture, her mind imagining the charcoal pencils and different types of paper she would need. "With a blender stump I would do the shading on this corner," she mutters, her head a little to one side, looking at the photograph thinking greyscale. She suddenly notices her finger on the picture. There isn't even a twitching in her finger and her whole body feels relaxed! Wait, she's thinking art...? She's really thinking colours and medium and blending and... and... She sits back in shock, needing to process that, but not wanting to go there, not now anyway. "I'd better drink my tea, just in case," she says, feeling an odd lightness in her heart, but firmly closing her mind on that too. Just when she puts her empty mug down, a young couple walk out onto the terrace, searching, looking round. Their faces light up when they see her, and Martha makes sure that her mouth is shaped in a large grin.

"Hi, you must be the holiday rep?"

The man has a light voice, matching his light blue eyes, Martha thinks, her grin not such a struggle just then. She nods and motions to the chairs in front of the table, closing the large folder at the same time.

29

The young couple sit down, still holding hands, glowing and energetic, clearly on top of the world. Not like Martha who struggles to keep some black tea and toast down, and who just spilled her tea and... She stops herself, forcing herself to focus on the couple, making eye contact, linking her fingers together under the table, squeezing the tension out.

"Yes, I am. My name is Martha Taylor. Now, how are you enjoying your holiday so far?" she asks, pushing her glasses up higher.

The couple assure her that the resort is everything they had hoped for.

"Is there anything you would like to know about?" she continues, feeling a slight tremor in her shoulders, worried that she will have no idea how to help these people. After all, this is her first time in Crete, she has only just arrived and has had limited time to go through the huge folder.

The young woman leans forward and explains that they would love to do something a bit more active.

Martha nods, hoping that she will remember the active options. After all, it's not the young couple's fault that she is new. They have paid for an expensive holiday, trusting the holiday rep to give them advice. That is what it says in the adverts, and Martha hasn't got an excuse for letting down the company. "There are a few options for something more active, although some of the outings are a little further away from the resort," she says, hoping it sounds professional enough, needing the few moments it will buy her to get the list sorted out in her head.

A quick floating image of the confident Joan – *or was it Jean?* – glides into her head, making her skip a few pages. The woman smiled at people, leaned back in her chair, chatted and waved her hands when explaining something. Martha swallows and tucks her hair behind her ear, resisting the urge to try out some hand gestures herself. For one thing, she hasn't got a clue what she'll say to accompany the gestures at this stage.

"We've been here a week now, and it's gorgeous and all that, but we'd like to do something a bit more challenging," the young woman says, and Martha nods as she lands back down to the here and now with a bump. Looking at the folder she finds her mind drifting to the beautiful photograph she was looking at just now.

"You see, we're both quite sporty normally, so a week of hanging around is lovely, but we're getting a bit itchy now," the young man explains.

Yes, Martha noticed that they both look like they enjoy exercise. She looks down at the folder, turning a few pages without seeing, fighting against a little green-eyed monster moving around. *I would love to get fit, to run or swim...* She gulps. *No, maybe not swim... Walking that gorge would be amazing though!* Although, she'd probably want to sit down at the first beautiful spot to paint or draw!

Martha's fingers automatically stop at the right information, and she turns the folder towards the couple. "Would this be something you would enjoy? It's strenuous though, especially in the heat. The Gorge is supposed to be spectacular, as you can tell just from this picture," she adds, and watches the two young people bend over the page with information. They quickly read it, and look at each other, leaning back with satisfied faces. "You can see, the pickup from here is at 5.30 in the

31

morning, and you'll be back very late that evening," Martha points out, thinking how personally she would dread a day like that!

A memory of a walk comes to her, not in sunny Crete, but in rain-drenched Cotswolds fields. Of course, the walk started when it was just a *little* overcast, but soon the walk went from bad to a lot worse. William blamed her, pointing out how her constant nagging about the countryside had made him take her out. He had not been able to check the weather properly because she had made him feel too guilty and put pressure on him – and she never gave him a moment's peace to get his bearings. He couldn't rely on *her* for that sort of thing, of course, even though Martha is still convinced that she mentioned the shape of the clouds and how that wasn't good news for a ramble. She was utterly exhausted and chilled to the bone by the time they got back, resulting in a terrible cold. Martha shudders – those days were terrifying, with her struggling to cough without making the slightest noise, to avoid William's wrath. No, walking would definitely not be her choice from all the options on the list. *That Gorge does look stunning though...*

"Just the thing," the man says, confident, smiling. "No worries about it being a hard thing to do; we've done lots of walking and the like. I know the heat is an issue – but yeah, we'll be fine!"

The young woman nods in agreement, leaning forward a bit more, reading more of the information.

Martha pulls out the spare leaflet tucked behind the front one and passes it to the young couple.

"We'll be tired..." The man grins at the young woman, and Martha can tell their excitement. "Can we book it via you?" he asks, looking at Martha. She nods and takes a clean paper. "Mr and Mrs Thomas," he says with a grin, and Martha wonders if he's always so happy, or whether it's their honeymoon, novelty making him that smiley.

She writes down their names, the number of the excursion, the day they would like to go, and the payment needed to be put to their holiday account. She double and triple checks all the information, dreading that she will forget something. She checks her own list provided by Jean... *No, Joan... Was it Joan?* Never mind – according to the list, she has got all the details necessary. She writes the day and time of pickup on the leaflet for Mr and Mrs Thomas.

"Thank you. You certainly are very neat and organised," Mr Thomas says, grinning, and Martha feels her hands go clammy. She pokes her glasses up higher, tucks her hair behind her ear and smiles broadly, linking her fingers together under the table, banning herself from worrying about that statement.

He probably means I look like I've got OCD, or am totally inept, she thinks, smile in place. *Why else would he say something like that in front of his wife?* She feels relieved when the couple say that this was all they needed.

"I will be here most days," Martha smiles, feeling her jaw beginning to lock up, "so if there is anything else later in the week, you're always welcome, of course. You have my number?" she checks, one eye on her checklist of dealing with clients. They nod, thank her and walk off, excited about their ridiculously long day.

Martha breathes out, feeling like a leaking inflatable. *What if I didn't write it down? Then I would forget, make mistakes and really mess up their day – or even their holiday,* she thinks, feeling judged and unable to defend herself. *Why did he say that anyway?* She stares across the now empty terrace, her dark blue eyes looking disturbed. She stops with her hand on the bit of hair that she was just tucking behind her ear again. "It's really getting greasy; what will people think? Why did I even touch it? I wonder if she noticed; they both looked so capable and in control," she sighs, the green-eyed monster having grown by the minute.

She doesn't notice the manager walking across the terrace, too busy with her brooding thought. Suddenly he sits down in one of the chairs, making Martha jump. Literally. He grins at her, a little sheepish.

"Sorry about this morning. My name is Mac. I'm the manager here. No doubt Joan told you that," he says, and chuckles.

Martha manages to nod, unable to breathe, large smile firmly in place, her fingers tracing the shape of her locket, comforted by its warmth.

"She probably told you I'm a real grouch as well," he continues, and chuckles again which turns into a rattling cough.

Martha smiles even more, starts to nod, realises that he probably doesn't want that one confirmed, so turns the nod into a shake, and stops, as she can't lie, can she? This really makes Mac laugh, and he coughs till his face is redder than normal. He breathes out at last, and Martha feels her grip on her smile slipping when the smell of his breath drifts across the table. She hides her hands, as they have started to shake noticeably, worried that she will not be able to hold it together much longer.

"Anyway," Mac, says, getting up with difficulty, "great to have you on board – and ignore my grumpy moments!"

Martha moves her head up and down, hoping it looks like she is nodding.

"If you need anything, I'm usually good at getting stuff sorted, so do ask. Hope you'll settle in and enjoy it." He nods and walks away, taking the smell of alcohol with him.

Martha sees him going down the terrace towards the pool, grabs her bag, and staggers into the dining room as fast as possible without looking as if she is trying to catch a bus – through the empty dining room, into the hall, and frantically into the ladies' bathroom, her stomach heaving, hand over her mouth, knowing that to be a futile gesture. She dives headlong into the nearest cubicle and is sick for the second time that day.

She leans against the door, having locked it, and breathes... and counts... and after what seems like too long, finds herself breathing calmly again. The tears are not so easily dealt with. "I can't do this. My first day and I've been sick twice, been laughed at and now this... I can't avoid Mac, can I? And I certainly can't make a dash for the bathroom every time I meet him! I will have to give up. I thought I was ready, but obviously I'm not. I will just have to go back..." Her voice trails off. Go back? Back to the Cotswolds to admit total defeat? Then do what? Moon around the house all day, rehashing her failure as holiday rep? "I was so sure I could take this step, so confident..." Martha feels trapped again, for what choice has she got? Has she made a terrible decision again by committing to this job? She can't leave here, and her sister will not be impressed if she turns up again after only one day on the job. "Maybe I should make a Failure CV," she says, tears steaming up her glasses. "Failed as wife, holiday rep – there'll be other things as well, I'm sure." Self-pity threatens to take over when she thinks back to the previous time she visited these facilities in a rush. Was that really only this morning?

Moments of today flit in and out of her mind: the cicada chirping away, the stunning colours, the warmth... the smiles that have been such gifts to her during this day. Martha lifts up her locket with both hands, and whispers through fresh tears, "Yes Lord, I can do it. I can do all things through Christ, even this... I will just need to..." She stops as she really has no idea how to overcome the obstacles she has encountered so far today! "I will overcome," she says, with a determined voice, then looks round her, startled, realising she is in a public place! The odd sound that used to be a giggle comes then, and Martha washes her face, grabs a new black tea, and heads back to her table, resolved to be a victor for the rest of the day. "I'm sure I'll manage that, seeing that most of the day has gone," she says, inhaling the salty smell from the nearby beach, the now almost familiar smile back.

5

MARTHA WAKES UP EARLY, RELIEVED THAT THE night has been uneventful. She debated for ages with herself about the previous night. "Do I lock the door and windows, then risk a nightmare because of the heat and stuffiness? Or do I risk a peaceful sleep knowing that my window is open?" After her night-time regime and careful putting out her clothes for the next morning, she sat down with her new journal and added, "Smiled today." She looked at the words, feeling pathetic. "What woman my age writes down as the largest blessing of her day, 'I smiled'?" she sighed. By then she felt hot already, so she decided to leave her window open. The side door to the kitchen was underneath her room, so a few times she jumped out of bed to check that the voices just underneath her window were definitely Greek-speaking. Each time, it was kitchen workers having a quick smoke and a chat, clearly trying to keep their voices down. Martha could just see the bottom part of the stairs leading up to her room and others along the same balcony. Nobody got near those steps, apart from one of the girls who just sat down on the bottom step for a few moments. After a while Martha felt too tired to get out of bed. She felt a little bit silly as well, knowing that she was being paranoid. The breeze from the open window was lovely though.

Now Martha lies back, waiting for her ten-minute snooze alarm to go. She feels relaxed, awake and at peace. She thinks about her journal entries, and for a few seconds lets her mind explore why she actually smiled yesterday. "Like now," she muses, "normally these ten minutes make me tense, feeling a proper rebel for not jumping out of bed at the first sound of the alarm. Now I'm just lying here, feeling... I don't know... feeling relaxed, I suppose..." A bird sings outside, she can just hear the waves gently licking at the shells, and she feels her mouth curving into a smile again. "I used to be like this," she whispers, suddenly feeling tears rushing up, but without the shaking. "I used to smile quite a lot, then I stopped." She stops her mind from going any further.

The sudden alarm is a relief, not because of her tense rebellion, but because it stops her from having to explore too much! Martha gets up, carefully following her routine, grateful for the sense of normalcy that it affords her. "I might be in a mess, but this is all neat and structured."

Breakfast is not as dauting as it was the day before, and Martha manages to smile her broad smile at various people, nodding especially at the young couple that she recognises, although she doesn't even try to remember their names. "Their names will be in my Lifeline," she says to herself, pouring the black tea and putting some toast and fruit on her plate. "There is that older couple. I saw them yesterday. Now, did they come and see me?" She smiles at them, her grimace a little more genuine, as she feels again that the couple gives her a safe feeling. She is disappointed when she discovers from her Lifeline that the older couple didn't come to see her yesterday. "I really thought they did; I remember her face so vividly; I even remember the colour dress she wore." Martha turns the pages of her notebook, just to double-check. *No, the young couple were the only ones. Oh, and Mac the manager, of course.* She doesn't need her notebook to remind herself of him; the smell of alcohol on his breath can be recalled at any time.

She purposefully inhales her black tea and realises with a tiny shock that her plate is empty! *I have actually eaten my breakfast already. Maybe I should get some more...* A sudden tightness stops her from getting up. *Maybe not. There will be baklava later on, no doubt, and that is very sweet.* In the far distance she can hear the Voice counting up all the foods she has had so far, his eyes taking in her body. She can still feel the heat, the feeling of shame, but also confusion and anger. She can't quite formulate what the anger is aimed at, and at the same time her head seems to shape images and incidents, rather than the blanket heat towards him that she got used to.

Martha looks across the dining room, holding the warm mug in both her slight, trembling hands. "Did I really eat both those cupcakes? I don't even like cake, so why did I eat them? He said it was because I had a food problem, that I was trying to draw attention to myself over food – but cupcakes? We looked, and found the wrappers in my little bin..." Tears blur her eyes, as she can still see herself standing there like a naughty schoolgirl, her husband – well, ex-husband – holding out the wrappers, his voice sympathetic, as he explained to his mum that she had "just some food issues". She ran to the bathroom then and was sick, but definitely not with cakes. *The wrappers, though...* Martha sighs, and forces the incident to go away, breathing in the warm tea and exhaling whilst counting in a calm inner voice. The Voice recedes, and all her eyes can see is blue sky and gorgeous artwork.

She hurries back to her studio using the large tiled path. The heat can already be felt radiating off the large flagstones. She takes in the soft, warm colours of the stones, very earthy colours like terra cotta. The large bushes along the path give some shade, as well as making it feel lush and like a welcoming resort. Through the gaps between bushes she can see the road, or even parts of the beach, and near her apartment she can see the little rocky inlet.

Martha gets back to her studio and sits at the table to look through her lists for the day. "Be available to answer questions or sort out alternative arrangements for people going to the Aquarium," she says, her finger tapping the paper. "That's at ten this morning." She looks at the clock on her wall. "That gives me another hour and a half." Martha looks at the folder and other papers. Somehow, she can't get motivated to look through the folder again to read all the possibilities and excursions on offer. She has spent all yesterday evening doing just that, and actually completed her list of options. "Maybe I should just go for a walk," she says out loud, then laughs scornfully, the sound actually scaring her! "That sounded like... Well, why *shouldn't* I go for a walk?" she says defensively. She looks at her door and feels the tightness return. The idea of *just* walking outside, and *just* walking off to goodness-knows-where makes her breath more rapid already. Martha sits very still, feeling her heartrate picking up, little panic flags waving at her, asking her how she had thought to do that? "Where would I go?" she wonders; then she remembers the blue sky, the beautiful shade of blue that the sea was, its gentle sound calming her, calling her.

She takes a deep breath, then pushes her chair back with a very determined motion. "That's it! I am going for a walk. It's my decision to make." She quickly puts her notebook in her handbag, takes the studio key from its usual spot, and manages to lock the door behind her in spite of her shaking hands. Her legs struggle going down the stairs, as if they're trying to persuade her that this is not a good idea... Martha manages to get downstairs though, and soon she has left Sapphire Seaside Resort and is on the promenade in front, forcing her legs to take smart, confident steps, praying that her knees won't suddenly rebel and buckle...

In minutes Martha finds herself walking on the actual beach, shells crunching softly underneath her sandals. Wherever she looks, there are sun-loungers and umbrellas, so she makes sure to keep her eyes on the blue sea. "Definitely Egyptian Blue," she smiles to herself, knowing full well that each wave seems to have a different shade than the last one!

There is a tiny empty spot between the sets of sun loungers, and Martha actually sits down on the warm sand, her fingers just feeling, rubbing, playing with the sand. "This is just so peaceful," she breathes, her eyes looking all over the sea in front of her. Not too far away is a large island, odd shapes of leftover mist making it look like a jigsaw puzzle that needs completing. The mists swirl a little in a breeze that also makes her wavy hair move – apart from the few strands firmly tucked behind her left ear, of course. Martha loves looking at the island. "All you'd need is greyscale pencils, different greens, and white and black of course," she thinks, looking at the island with her head tilted. "I love doing rocks, they feel so solid, so enduring," she realises suddenly. This brings another soft smile, and she can almost feel the weight of a beautiful pencil in her hand. Her shoulders start their immediate protest and her mind is quick to join. "I don't think I can; I don't think I ever can," she says softly, and is immediately overwhelmed with a feeling of disappointment, as though her heart has slumped down, filled with loss. "I mean, what if I..." She stops, suddenly demanding, "What if I *what?* Why shouldn't I? Who is there to stop me, apart from..." She swallows, feeling that she might go too far, taunt life too much, but bravely finishes her own question. "What is to stop me apart from *memories?*" Her eyes glide over the water; noticing its clearness and how she can see the grey stones underneath the surface; noticing the white flecks dancing when the waves splatter onto the beach, the sun dancing on each separate drop... "I *need* to," she says, half-aloud. "I just *need* to – and I *will!*" She feels her smile growing, and the odd noise that is meant to be a giggle rasps out. Yes, her smile is definitely a broad one, but this time the smile is real, effortless, and her whole body joins in.

Martha is back only just in time to see the clients off on their organised excursion. The bus driver's loud voice on the phone makes her shrink inside a little, but the euphoric feeling at having made the monumental decision to draw again sees her through. She's amazed by her own calmness around the bus driver, as normally a voice and attitude like that would make her shrink and shrivel inside, and she'd be shaking! She nods and smiles at the clients getting on the coach, and answers a few questions that an older lady and her friend ask her. She pushes her glasses up, tugs at her hair, feeling unnerved by so many people around her. A male voice behind her is nearly her undoing. "Sorry, I didn't see you," she gasps, pretending to apologise for blocking the man's path, even though he had no reason to walk up behind her! The man hardly notices her, too busy telling his wife and a friend about the tropical fishing trips he has been on and all the fish he would recognise at the drop of a hat... Martha shuffles a little further away from the coach, her shaking hand round her hot locket.

A few more people are marked on her list, then Martha walks over to the driver who has by now finished his very loud conversation. "I think that is everyone," she says, feeling the heat on her face grow as she watches how the list shakes and shudders in her hands. The bus driver nods, not looking too interested at all, takes the list out of her hands without noticing how shaky they are, nods at her again, then grunts something that could have been in English or Greek or any language for that matter. Martha swallows, locking her fingers together tightly, smiling broadly, telling herself that lots of people grunt. *He definitely did not smell of alcohol,* she tries to reason with herself, knowing that trying to use logic on herself doesn't always work very well. *Maybe his English isn't that great, and he just feels awkward speaking English, or – well – he might have all sorts of reasons.* She realises that she is wasting her energy. The man grunted at her – no big deal. This stern voice reminds her of her brother-in-law, who is

Mr Reasonable himself. Martha waves the coach off, then finds herself back in her studio in no time.

Her hands are shaking but this time with excitement! She packs her handbag carefully: Lifeline, phone, holiday rep phone, bus timetable, map of Iraklion... She looks round her very neat studio, trying to remember what else she will need for her shopping trip. Then she suddenly drops down, pulls out her stout notebook and makes her list, knowing that her nerves will take over by the time she gets to the bus stop. "Get to the bus, the bus to Iraklion. Find the less touristy area Joan mentioned, buy art book, buy paper and pencils. Get back to the bus station, get the bus to Sapphire Seaside Resort. Now, as for the type of paper and colour pencils to get..." She stops, her mind pulling and pushing at her. "What pencils?" she whispers, realising that somehow she can't say the colours, the shades, and it scares her. "Breathe, just breathe!" She pauses for a moment, then says, "The decision is made. I am not changing my mind. I will buy pencils, and I will buy the right paper. I will choose whatever colours I think I will need. This is my decision; I'm a victor and I will choose." This helps, and Martha soon finds herself, map in trembling hands, walking slightly uphill along a dusty road on her way to a Cretan bus stop.

6

IRAKLION HITS MARTHA HARD. THE HEAT AND
the noise make her gasp, and her legs simply refuse to step
away from the bus. Her shoulders cramp together, her
arms start to shake, and Martha knows that it's mere
minutes before her whole body will let her down. She
scans the area round the busy, noisy bus station and spots
a small bench in a shady spot to the side of the station.
She wobbles across to the bench as fast as her trembling
legs will let her and drops down onto it. She turns away a
little from the busyness, tilting her face up to the high city
wall, and rolls with the panic. Her body is shaking, tears
splatter down, but in the heat they are almost dried up
before they reach her chin. Martha tries to make her inner
voice louder than the humming, buzzing noise in her ears,
louder than her rasping frantic breaths, and counts, telling
herself between counts to breathe in... and out...
reminding herself through tears that she is not a victim,
but a victor, and that she can do all things – yes, *all* things,
even extreme things like coping with heaving bus stations
in a foreign city.

After a while the inner voice is definitely on the home
streak, and Martha manages to remove her glasses, pats
them dry on a tissue, wipes her eyes and blows her nose,
breathing, counting, and suddenly feeling impatient with

it all. She takes some extra deep breaths, then pulls out her Lifeline to check why on earth she has made this trip.

It must have been something urgent or important for me to get on a bus in this heat to go to a big city! She turns to the last page, staring at her writing. *I came this way, went through all this… to buy pencils?* She stares around the bus station, feeling as if she somehow has missed something very obvious. She turns back to her notebook. *Paper and pencils and art books. Really?* She unfolds the map of Iraklion and works out which way to go from here. There is a marked area and an arrow leads to the words "art books and galleries" scribbled in the sideline. "Well, as I went through all that effort to get here, I'd better go and see the area," she mutters, still in shock that she got herself into this!

The little streets with quiet shops are just what she needs though. Martha finds herself breathing fast again, this time with excitement and an overwhelming feeling that just revels in all the beautiful things she sees everywhere. She looks at some of the paintings, carefully touching some of them. "Oil, and nicely done too!" Pottery isn't really her thing but some of the collections have such incredible colours that she is still drawn in. Then there is a shop that has books, prints, cards and all kinds of pictures. Martha looks through the books, shocked by some of the prices. Near the back are some smaller books with different kinds of art. One has a large painting of an amphora on the front, a large jar, almost like a vase, its two handles sticking out like little round ears on either side. She turns a few of the pages, and gulps. "There is the painting from the hotel," she whispers, feeling pleased. She turns the book over, and the price on the back makes her feel even better, as this one is definitely within her budget! She selects a book from lower down the stack and takes it to the small desk.

The man behind the cash register grins at her, showing a gold tooth in one corner. "This one, please," Martha says, showing her broad grin, hoping the man will be quick. She feels uncomfortable in the little shop, too hot all of a sudden. The man doesn't seem to be in a hurry at all, making Martha squirm inside. Finally, she is holding the book, wrapped in a little paper bag, receipt in her other hand, and she almost flees the shop. Back in the little cobblestoned, narrow alleyway she feels a bit silly.

Does that mean I'm done? So back to the bus? she wonders, something nagging in the back of her mind as she slowly carries on. In the end she pulls out her notebook to check. "Pencils! Of course," she says out loud, making an older woman stare at her with piercing, black eyes.

Just when she gets to the end of the marked area, Martha spots the shop. It's small and dark, but Martha only has eyes for the rows and rows of coloured pencils. With shaking hands, she pulls her handbag higher up her shoulder, jabs her glasses on the little gold bridge, and tucks her hair behind her ear, her eyes never leaving the pencils. She somehow remembers the list: greyscale, greens, black and white, paper and putty. Her eyes shining, Martha walks over to a large section of all things green. Her fingers trace the different types of green, wondering which ones to get. *Olive green, jade green, probably the yellow green as well as lime green? Mmmm... I don't really like the lime one; it's too bright. A black and a white, and now for grey. Cool grey and pale rose which will be beautiful for lots of the rocks.* Martha can feel her mind buzzing with a thrill that seems to belong to another lifetime, another world. *I haven't felt like this for... for ages,* she ends quickly, wanting to hang on to the pleasant feeling, rather than analyse it. *Now for some paper.* This is almost as exciting as the colours, but in the end, Martha makes her way to the till with a few sketchpads in different shapes and sizes, her pencils, some putty and a pencil sharpener. The woman at the corner desk smiles at her, and Martha notices her kind eyes. The woman seems very young, and Martha is happy to answer her question.

"I wanted to draw the island opposite the resort," she explains, imagining the feeling of these brand-new pencils gliding across the paper already.

"Ah, you mean the larger island?" the young woman asks. "It is called Dia. It is not very large, but very interesting. Tourists often visit it for the day. There is nobody living there, not now anyway. There are some remains of people – you know, houses – so in ancient times they did live there. Now the Kri-Kri live there, the special goat." She smiles, her voice melodically sweet and rich, calming Martha as well as making her feel excited.

The girl makes the little explanation sound like a story, and Martha can imagine her telling stories, or being on a stage, enthralling her audience with her warm voice. She thanks the young woman for her information and explains that she is staying at the Sapphire Seaside Resort as the holiday rep, but that she has most of today off.

"Oh, my brother sometimes has people from that resort. He has a boat," the woman says. "His name is Dimitris. We live in the town a bit further along the coast.

It is a bigger town so many people come to the hotels and tavernas there. My brother has a boat, and he takes tourists out on the water. He goes to Dia, where they walk and swim, and then he brings them back in the afternoon. He likes it and has many people doing it."

Martha quickly gets her notebook out and asks the woman to write down her brother's name and information for her. "My clients often ask for local trips and days out," she explains, "so it would be nice to have something to recommend."

The young woman nods and carefully writes down "Dimitris Floros". "My name is Anna Floros," she tells Martha, while writing down the address and information of Dimitris' job. Martha thanks her, glad that Anna wrote the information in English, not using the Greek alphabet... She puts her notebook away, feeling reluctant to leave the young woman. She really likes Anna and would like to know more about her.

Almost as though she could read her mind, Anna picks up a small business card and gives it to Martha. "This is the address of our church," she smiles, studying Martha's face. "It's an international church, so everything is in English, and sometimes in Russian as well. Our pastor is from Ukraine – Pastor Volodya. You will be very welcome if you want to come."

Martha stares at the little card in her hand, swallows, and looks back at Anna. She can feel tears growing in her eyes, blurring her vision, and she tries to blink them away. She almost puts on her large smile but stops herself. She somehow knows that with Anna the large smile is not necessary.

"Um... thank you," she says, and hesitates before adding suddenly, "I would like to come, I really would. It's just that... I... um... I struggle a little at the moment. I know God does what is best for us; it's just that I seem to have a different opinion of what best is for me... This last year has been... horrible – *really* horrible – and I still struggle." She looks at Anna, who nods, her very dark eyes looking serious but very kind. "I suppose I just want prayers answered quicker than they usually are," Martha adds, then stops and smiles suddenly. "Although, God used a cicada the other night rather promptly to pull me out of a panic attack," she admits, and the giggle that follows isn't nearly as rough as they have been. It sounds quite a natural giggle in fact.

Anna laughs as well and agrees that even a cicada could probably be put to some good use somewhere!

"I would like to go," Martha finds herself saying. "I really would. I have missed church, actually, and I miss God too." She smiles sadly at Anna, feeling her eyes burning, but relieved to have spoken the words out loud, stunned to find herself connecting and opening up to a stranger! Somehow a connection has been made between them, between her and all her fears and this unknown Cretan young woman. It feels just right though, and Martha locks it away to think about and enjoy another time. Anna takes the little card back, and quickly scribbles her number on the back. "Text me; we can pick you up at 9.30 from your hotel," she smiles, and hands the card back to Martha.

Martha thanks her and they agree that Anna and Dimitris will pick her up this Sunday morning. Martha knows that if she doesn't agree to the arrangement now, it will just never happen. The idea of texting someone to ask to be picked up is making her heart beat faster already!

They say goodbye, and once Martha is out of the shop, she unfolds the map, feeling exhausted beyond belief. The city has some lovely little corners, but Martha just wants to get back to the bus station, back to the resort.

Somehow, she makes it back to the station, her legs protesting, her shirt stuck to her back, every yard feeling like a half-marathon. The bus driver grunts when she double-checks the route, but Martha is too tired to even react to the grunt! *Or maybe I'm no longer triggered by grunts,* she hopes.

The walk back to the resort almost has her in tears. The heat, the dust and the seemingly endless track are too much. "I can do all things, even talking to strangers, agreeing to go back to a church, and wandering around in the heat. I most certainly am a victor, although I'll soon be a victim to this heat if I don't get back to the studio soon," she mutters, fighting tears, her inner voice sternly commanding the Voice to stay out of it all.

7

MARTHA SINKS DOWN ON HER BED WITH relief. "I made it!" She soon gets up again to put her pencils and paper away and sort out her handbag. She puts the art book on her shelf, then pours herself a drink which she takes to the balcony. It feels good just sitting down in the shade, watching the sea and Dia island. She can feel her fingers twitching, eager to start on the drawing, but she resists.

Martha sighs, feeling her shoulders tightening up just thinking about drawing again. "You're so weak," the Voice hisses in her mind. *"What's the point of buying these pencils, knowing that you're unable to make your own decisions?"* The Voice taunts her into defiance, for actually, Martha has made quite a few decisions the last few days! She documented them too in her Lifeline, which is exactly what that notebook is for. Martha would never have thought that she would answer back to the Voice, ever! A few days ago, the mere thought of doing so would make her physically sick; now she just feels indignation.

"I decided to buy pencils and paper, and I have decided to draw Dia, and I will. Not today though. I have been pushed out of my comfort zone enough for one day," she tells herself, feeling a little feeble for postponing her drawing. On the other hand, deciding to draw another day is a decision too, and a valid one at that! Anyway, this evening light is not the right light for her; she prefers the island in the morning light, its colour more vibrant and sharply outlined. The evening is beautiful, but softer, like someone has used a blending implement to blend the colours, smoothing out the edges. She remembers the feelings of the warm sand gliding through her fingers and feels an unusual longing for the morning.

Martha looks at her notebook, reading the page she has written in the bus. *I liked Anna. She seems very kind. I hope her brother is too...* She has a fleeting image of the loud bus driver but shakes her head to clear the image. *Hopefully the brother will look like Anna,* she continues, carefully checking Anna's number and copying it from the little card into her notebook. The special hotel phone rings and Martha answers it. One of the clients wants to know the name and website of the water park, so Martha finds it for them. That call seems to trigger other calls, and the rest of the afternoon Martha is busy seeing and helping clients. Dinnertime finds her quite hungry, which surprises her.

The dining room is very full, but there are still spaces outside, which Martha prefers anyway. She walks past the buffet, only taking a little bit here and there, but her face lights up when she spots the baklava in the pudding section! Her hand hovers over the tray. She really, really wants two pieces, but will people think her greedy? Will they comment about diets and all that? She can hear the Voice coming closer, the posh voice loud and clear in the distance, and without hesitation Martha grabs two large pieces of baklava. "I'm not overweight. According to the charts my BMI is actually low, so I'm definitely allowed some baklava," she mutters, then quickly walks to an outside table to avoid giving in and putting a piece back!

She finds herself enjoying her meal, able to ignore most of the noise around her. Once or twice she stiffens, almost dropping her cutlery when a man calls out across the terrace, but Martha feels that today has actually been a good day, better than she expected. She pulls her Lifeline out of her bag, adding the two pieces of baklava as well as a reasonable dinner to the list. Martha looks at the gooey baklava sitting on her plate in a little sticky honey puddle, and she suddenly pulls her phone from her bag and takes a picture. She clicks on her sister's number and sends the picture, adding, "Have arrived, it's going well," then stops. Should she add, "Bought pencils and paper," or would that be asking for trouble? Will telling her sister make her back away from actually drawing Dia, feeling the pressure? In the end she decides to leave it. *I could send her a picture once I have started,* she decides.

That evening Martha writes in her blessing journal with a smile. It's been a day of blessings, really. Most days she has to dig deep to find one blessing to write down; this evening she has a whole list to choose from. Staring at the day and date, she suddenly smiles. "Why not? I'm the one in charge," she says, then looks over her shoulder briefly, as if she expects somebody to contradict her. Even the Voice decides not to argue that point for now. "As I'm in charge," she repeats, because it's such a liberating statement, "I get to set the rules. There isn't a rule that it can only be one blessing each day. The one blessing rule only came in because – well, because most of the time finding just one blessing was hard enough! Today I can actually really count my blessings one by one." She smiles and giggles, pleased with the genuine sound it is turning into. Then she picks up her pen and writes a long list of blessings, feeling each one all over working in her heart, blessing her anew, making her smile grow – and something in her heart seems to... *change*. She puts her pen down, looking around her, still smiling, but also a tiny bit curious about this feeling. "I feel much more relaxed," she whispers. "I find myself smiling all through the day, and my panic attacks seem shorter lived than they used to be. I got all through the day without being sick." She pulls a face at that, but still, it's a change – a good one too.

Her phone beeps; it's a message back from her sister. "Good for you, looks delicious! Glad you're doing well, keep in touch! Xx."

Martha smiles, and feels a change towards her sister as well. They actually exchanged texts like... like normal sisters! "Alright, I didn't tell her about drawing again because of my fear of pressure, but this was quite a step as well. She responded in a sweet way; I have missed that!" Tears sting suddenly. Martha runs indoors, shutting the door quickly behind her, and throws herself on the bed like a teenager in despair. And she cries. She sobs and groans for ages, and when she finally calms down, she sits on the edge of the bed, drying her face. "I have missed all that time with my sister. I can never get those years back, and only now do I really see what I have missed out on. I closed my mind to that loss, ignored it, pretended all was well. I knew it wasn't. Now we're actually talking again, and I can see the gap and that our relationship will need healing too." She sighs. So much to make up for, so much to repair, and some of it will be beyond repair. Martha feels forlorn, new tears burning, her shoulders tightening as she thinks about the long road ahead. It feels so overwhelming, and it seems that each time she makes a tiny positive change, other things happen to show how much still needs to be healed. "Will I ever get there, and is it even worth the effort?"

She looks at her phone, remembers her sister's hurt and anger over what was done to her – her empathy and care – and she takes a deep, deep breath. "One step at a time." She smiles a little, as her sister kept telling her that too: "One step is all you can take." Then she thinks about the long list of blessings and feels something that seems very similar to confidence. Of course, it can't be confidence, for she has none. No courage either, she thinks, but then, she got on a bus, went to a strange city, sort of coped with lots of noise and people, bought a book, talked to a stranger and arranged to be picked up for church...

Martha gulps. *Church!* She'd forgotten about that! "I'm going to a church on Sunday, one that I have never been to, and the only person that I will recognise is a young woman I talked to in a shop..." Her breathing speeds up in sympathy, and Martha can feel panic flags being raised. "I'm not a victim," she whispers desperately, "I'm a victor, and I can do all things through Christ who strengthens me... I can even walk into a new church all by myself without passing out or being sick all over the floor..." That mental image helps somehow, and Martha finds herself pulling a face, thinking about all the possible ways her church visit could go wrong. Somehow, instead of coming up with very real and possible disasters, her mind must have suffered from the heat. *I might get my hand trapped in their collection bag... I might sing in the toilet and be heard...* She giggles, the sudden noise making her jump, but somehow she has overridden the panic attack!

Martha gets up, feeling the moment, accepting the tiny shift inside her, and from her bottom drawer pulls a large new notebook. It's not really her style, the colours too bright and gaudy, but her sister bought it for her. "To record your steps, one by one," she smiled, her eyes full of tears and sadness, trying to pass on hope; willing Martha to believe there would be steps forward, that healing was possible, that happiness could still be found. Martha promised to take it with her, so she did, but she put it in her drawer as soon as she arrived. After all, what was there to report? *Been sick twice? Keep forgetting people's names and whether or not I have actually met them? Need to make moment by moment lists, otherwise I don't even remember what my job title is?* Now, today, her heart has received a little colour though. The bleakness, the heavy mist, seems to have ripped a little, allowing the first pencil strokes in colour through.

Martha opens the book at the first page, her fingers tracing her sister's writing, words she has kept blocked out as they hurt too much. She quickly turns to the second page and writes the date at the top – and begins. First slowly, then faster and smoother as words just come. About that smile, that very first smile. About watching the island Dia, and her wish to draw again. Her bus trip, the shops, Anna and the invite to church. How she accepted the invite, made the arrangement. The text to her sister, and the tears that came along with realisation of lost times. Martha writes and cries, and writes some more. In the end she looks up, feeling that odd sensation of change again, too tired to explore any more for now.

It is later than usual, making her jittery, feeling a rule has been broken, but no panic flags are allowed to stay up. Martha forces them all down, putting her papers and notebooks away carefully, setting out her clothes for the morning, getting ready the way she always does, checking the door and windows. Then she sinks into her pillow with a sigh that could really be called one of contentment, which scares her more than the open window.

8

MARTHA IS GLAD THAT THE NEXT DAYS HELP
to establish a routine, a structure. Her 'blessing journal'
usually has more than one thing each evening, and the
notebook from her sister has been used each day. "I'm not
sure where this is going to lead to," she mumbles Saturday
evening, after scribbling away in her notebook for a while.
"Today was a busy day; I'm tired, and I can't remember
the last time I was tired like this. A normal, healthy tired."
She is sitting out on her little balcony, looking at the very
dark blue water, the waves still lapping away at the beach
nearby. The mountains are no longer visible, but Martha
hesitates to go inside. "I just feel different, but then, each
time I think I have overcome, or at least come a long way,
something happens. It's bound to happen this time.
Probably tomorrow! This church, all those new people,
Anna's brother... There is bound to be something to bring
me back down."

Martha can feel the brighter colours in her heart
shrinking, the darkness replacing some of them. "It's been
going so well these few days, I should have known it was
too good to be true," she mutters, then realises that she is
actually taking her downfall tomorrow as a given. This
makes her sit up, and she actually blushes in the dark, glad
to be alone! She knows that her attitude is very wrong,

and that by thinking like that, she'll cause it to happen, probably!

Martha looks at her sister's notebook again, knowing what she has written the last few days, and she knows that this is part of the problem. She is afraid of all the blessings, worried that they will run out, scared to feel rejected and hurt again, so she is trying to pre-empt that by expecting it. She is trying to get her head to be ready, to prevent herself from getting a nasty shock when these good times come to an end. "Nobody can be on the way up all the time," she reasons. "Doesn't matter how high your mountain is, you've got to come down sometime. Surely, it's better to be prepared for it..." Something feels wrong though, and Martha is too afraid to explore that for now. She is really worried about the morning, and she knows that her fear is making her look at things from the wrong perspective.

On an impulse she picks up her phone and sends her sister a text: "Going to International Church tomorrow... Please pray." Her sister will know the weight behind these simple words; she will understand her feelings this evening.

Soon her phone beeps and she smiles. It's one of the things she really appreciates about her sister: she always responds quickly. Her smile wavers when she remembers another particular time when they communicated very quickly – the main reason that she is able to sit here this evening. She reads her sister's response: "Brilliant! Thinking of you! Hugs, xxx."

Martha is slower in her bedtime routine this evening. Setting out her clothes for the morning seems a huge problem, and for a moment she wonders if she could use it as an excuse. The idea of having to contact Anna to cancel seems worse though.

Finally, there is no reason not to go to bed, yet Martha still hesitates. "I'm bound to have a nightmare tonight," she says. "I don't think I can go to sleep." She looks out through the curtains, hearing the cicadas arguing with the bright stars and the soothing noise from the sea. She smiles. "That is how I feel! Arguing in my head against so many good things, just out of fear." Then she remembers a prayer to keep evil away from our dreams, and sighs. "Maybe I should trust God to keep me safe, even when I close my eyes. I know in the daytime I look for ways to feel safe and to protect myself. At night I feel vulnerable, and it's lack of trust." She pulls a face, her mind just as quickly listing all the reasons why she should feel the way she does, making excuses and pointing in one very definite direction. She agrees, but the light-coloured bits in her heart seem to turn their mouths down in disapproval. Martha sighs again. "This is too complex, I'm too tired; I just hope I will sleep so I can handle tomorrow." She slowly walks over to her bed, still reluctant, adding, "I bet I have a terrible night, just to test me and to show me that change doesn't come that easily." Before the cicada outside has finished his tirade, Martha is asleep.

She wakes up in the morning feeling refreshed, as well as guilty for her surprise at having slept so well. Martha carefully follows her routine, trying to avoid thinking about the church and the people she will meet today. "I'm not a victim," she keeps repeating. "I can do all things..." Breakfast is half a piece of toast and some black tea, and even that feels like a huge Sunday roast in her stomach!

Martha shields her face from the sun, whilst looking for the car that will pick her up. Finally, an old car appears, light blue, mostly faded. A young man is driving, making her heart skip a few beats. Sapphire rings and Joan's laughing voice creep back into her memory. Funny how her mind seems to have no problem remembering comments like that...

Anna waves at her and hops out of the car once her brother has stopped. "Martha, so glad to see you again! Come, let me get the door for you," she says, her very dark eyes smiling with their kind glow, making Martha's shoulders stop their shaking.

Martha climbs into the car and says good morning to Dimitris, feeling nervous, but he seems to have the same kind eyes as Anna, and soon the three of them are on their way to Iraklion.

Anna asks about her pencils and paper, and Martha finds herself describing the start she made, just an outline really, of Dia Island.

"Those pencils are great," she smiles at Anna. "Their colours are quite soft, so easy to blend. I managed to get the grey just the way I wanted, so yes, I'm really enjoying it!" She doesn't explain how she measures her pencils every night. After all, who does? The shock she had one morning when she found her favourite pencil set sharpened down to almost nothing... Her husband explained to their visitors that she had an obsession with the pencil sharpener – OCD really. She stared at him in horror; not once did she remember sharpening her pencil set, apart from occasionally just a little, just to make the tip sharp! She must have done it whilst unaware – and even though she now suspects he made it all up, and in fact did it himself, she still doesn't feel sure. So every night she measures her pencils, just to make sure...

Talking to Anna about art and drawing and colours makes the trip to Iraklion go fast.

Parking near the church is difficult and Martha finds herself pleased with each minute Dimitris has to search for a space. "I know it's just putting it off," she says to herself, "and I will be fine; I am an overcomer, I'm a victor." Getting out of the car she notices that her freezing hands don't want to cooperate, and in spite of the heat rolling off the white houses along the street, she shivers.

The city is noisy, even in this part, and Martha spots the church building on their left, across the street. There are a few people milling about outside, some children are running up and down the steps, and she can feel her body turning the shiver into a shake.

Anna smiles at Martha. "Why don't you just stay with me? It's hard going into a new place, I always think." Her smile is kind and warm, as usual, and Martha is amazed to feel her body responding. The shakes smooth out and she finds that she can even move her fingers! Dimitris shakes hands with a man, ending the firm handshake in a man hug, and raises his chin at Anna.

"He's sitting with all his friends," Anna says, smiling back at her brother. "He usually does, as it's hard for him to find time to spend with them. Most of his friends have busy summer jobs. Dimitris is busy as well; the boat takes up a lot of time, as he needs to have it ready each morning. Some boat trips don't come back till almost evening!"

Martha looks at the laughing young men and tries to smile.

"Sometimes I go with him," Anna explains. "It's so beautiful on the water. The colours are gorgeous; I use them for my painting."

Martha's smile is real this time; she loved the pictures Anna showed her in the car. Anna paints abstract art, more a colour study than art, Martha thinks now, but the colours were incredible, and somehow the swirling, looping, flowing shapes had drawn her in.

"I just love to base my paintings on real life colour combinations," Anna says, her dark eyes dreaming away, probably out on the water in her brother's boat.

Martha is grateful for Anna's presence in the service. Pastor Volodya is a bit older than she expected, his Ukrainian accent strong, almost as strong as his handshake. She winces when he shakes her hand and welcomes her to the service. Singing familiar hymns helps, her hands almost a normal temperature now, and the reading calms her even more. He reads about the Shepherd who will feed His flock; He will carry them in His bosom, and gently lead those that are with young. She can hear her heart beating loudly, as if agreeing with Pastor Volodya, when he explains how we think we're strong, carrying many burdens and responsibilities; feeling that we are irreplaceable, and people depend on us, making us seem more important than we really are. Pastor Volodya shakes his head and smiles his broad grin, showing many gold teeth, which draw Martha's eyes like her light draws the mosquitos every night! Pastor Volodya shows how it's God that carries us; we're not ultimately in control, we're not in charge. "You cannot change another person," he says, "you can only work on yourself. You are responsible for your actions, your thoughts and your words. We still need to remember that we are like sheep, easily going astray, not able to look after ourselves, prone to wander off from all good things provided to us by our Shepherd." Martha's mind drifts away to the Cotswolds, where sheep seem to be everywhere – the green hills showing the white dots all around the farms, and their little quivering voices floating on the warm spring air.

After the service Anna takes Martha to meet a few of the other young women, and Martha finds her smile almost genuine. The women seem to come from all over Europe, and Martha soon forgets who is who, but they are friendly, and make her feel welcome.

Dimitris turns up too soon, she feels, but when she gets into the car, she realises how tired she is! The whole service has taken it out off her, leaving her drained, and her hands tremble from exhaustion. It feels good though, and she smiles at the passing trees and bushes.

Martha vaguely registers that Dimitris speaks to Anna is a low voice, in Greek and very seriously. Her mood swings round. *Are they talking about me?* she wonders, *Did I do something wrong? Maybe they regret taking me; I'm so boring, and I can't even remember anybody's name! I know one woman came from Norway. Or was it Sweden?* She feels the tension crawling into her, sticking her with sharp darts.

Anna suddenly turns round, her eyes softening when she looks at Martha.

9

"SORRY. DIMITRIS IS JUST WORRIED," ANNA says.
"One of the German lads says there have been thefts
locally – you know, old things, old Cretan things, like
pottery." Her face is serious, and Martha feels guilty for
her relief – relieved that they weren't talking about her
after all! "Dimitris says it's a problem, as those arts can
only be sold on properly, whereas stolen things sell on the
black market. There will be no certificate with them to
show that it's genuine ancient pottery, but some sellers
fake the papers. This makes it hard to stop the theft. It is
very sad, because our country is gradually losing its
heritage through this kind of criminal activity."

Martha nods, knowing how important it is to have
proof of any work of art.

"We don't know where it happens," Anna explains
after Dimitris says something in his low voice, still
sounding upset. "Dimitris says his friends think it's from
along the coast, but they aren't sure either. All they know
is, it is pottery and there has been some coming into the
market quite regularly. The person doing it might have
found an old site or shipwreck or something, and he is
slowly emptying it all out onto the black market."

Dimitris smiles at Martha in the mirror and shrugs his
shoulders. "Not to worry, Martha; they will catch him,

sometime in the next ten years, I think! I hope you like the resort? You like our beaches?"

Dimitris obviously wants to lighten the mood, and Martha smiles at this, thinking how kind they both are! Here he is, clearly upset by the theft issues, and yet he is trying to divert the conversation away from it to cheer her up. She nods at him, grateful, and explains that she hasn't been in the water yet...

Dimitris is shocked, "Oh, Martha! You must! The water – well, it truly is amazing! So warm and clear, you can see all the way down. Can you swim?"

Martha blushes a little, having to admit that she really ought to have gone into the water. The thought of the crowded beach makes her cringe though. She describes the beaches to Dimitris and Anna, and Anna laughs.

"I agree," Dimitris says, and he gives a very dramatic shudder, then says, "When you pass the little stream on the other side of the resort, follow the dusty road. It will soon come to a tiny harbour, and just beyond the harbour is the perfect beach for you. Some days you will find nobody there. *Nobody at all,* as there are no facilities." He nods encouragingly at her, as if he expects her to argue. Martha doesn't dream of arguing; the idea of a quiet, deserted beach sounds just perfect! "The resort is named after that beach, in fact," he adds. "Although most people assume the Sapphire Beach is the one in front of the resort, it isn't. Sapphire Beach is the one I just told you about; it's the perfect name for it."

Martha forces her mind away from images of rings with large sapphires set amid diamonds... and promises Anna and Dimitris to try out Sapphire Beach and to let them know next Sunday what it was like.

"The following week I will take you and Anna on my boat," Dimitris grins. "This week is very busy; there is a very large hotel in our town that has booked me for different groups. The following week is different."

Martha is sad to see her new friends drive away from Sapphire Seaside Resort, and waves, looking forward to the following week. She quickly writes the information about Sapphire Beach and plans for next week in her Lifeline, as well as a note about the stolen artefacts, as it might be of interest to some of her clients. She smiles at her schedule for the coming days. The picture of an empty stretch of golden sand hugged by sapphire blue sea sounds too wonderful for words!

In her journal she writes, "Looking forward, feeling excited about this beach. Daring to be pleased and anticipate something good." She surprised herself when she accepted Dimitris' offer to go out on the boat! "Fancy me going out on the water with people I have only just met!" Martha feels an odd thrill, and for a second she allows herself to imagine what William would think of her new freedom, but she doesn't let her mind go that way too far. She knows what he would think and say, and probably even do to her, and Martha just wants to bask in this new light, this light of freedom and joy that is spreading itself inside.

Martha really struggles with the ten minutes snooze option the following morning. *It's not fear this time, it's not needing to obey promptly, but I can't wait.* In the end, fear of leaving her structure behind makes her wait. Breakfast is rather rushed, and back in her studio Martha finally stops. "Do I wear a swimsuit?" She looks out of her window at the glistening waves, hearing the water washing over the stones, feeling it tugging at her heart strings. "The sea looks so inviting, and if there is really absolutely nobody there, then why not? I'm just not sure that there *will* be nobody there," she says, looking at her swimsuit, her shoulders tight. "What if I'm in the water and people turn up? I won't be able to get out..." She fingers the stretchy material, longing to be in the warm water, to watch the stones down deep, clearly to be seen through the clean water.

Martha takes a deep breath, then quickly gets changed. "I *will* wear it, and I'll see what it's like when I get there," she says out loud, then smiles at her attitude. "I will actually decide on the spot," she says, feeling very pleased with another little step. *Well, not so little, but still, by taking these steps they might begin to feel small and common.* She packs her suntan cream, towel and all things necessary, like her Lifeline. Martha packs and repacks her beach bag several times, realising that she is very nervous. "What do I even need?" she asks in the end, her arms shaking just a little as her body is realising that she is out of her depth, even before she gets to the water. After a while she gives up, and just packs what she hopes will be the essentials and leaves the rest out.

She is glad of her water bottle, as her mouth is very dry, her legs wobbling a little as she walks round the stream, then along the dusty road. There's not a car in sight, and it's very quiet, apart from some cicadas who sound as if they are trying to convince her that she is definitely not alone... The heat from the road is intense, but Martha's hands are freezing. She is looking forward to this beach, but her whole body shrieks at her to turn back – back to the resort, to normality, to routine, to safety. Martha, however, is determined to explore, to allow herself a little freedom, just one step out of her comfort zone. "There is the harbour. Should I turn back now and try this tomorrow? I don't think I can do this…" She thinks of Anna's kind eyes, Dimitris' smile and clear directions, and Pastor Volodya's sermon, telling them to rely on the Lord… Swapping her beach bag to her other hand, she mutters, "I can do all things and I'm not a victim."

The idea of taking off her dress and walking to the water in just her swimsuit makes her legs wobble more than ever. She manages to get past the small, empty harbour, and then she can see the beach!

Martha gasps, and stops. Soft, golden sand is spread out in a shape vaguely representing a crescent, the dark turquoise waters gently wandering onto the sand before hastily retreating. She stares, drinking in the rich colours, the warmth toned down with the slightest breeze coming off the water. Slowly she walks over to the beach, leaving the dusty road to walk onto the soft sand. Shrivelled and dried seaweed makes a low barrier and crunches softly under her sandals.

Once she gets onto the sand, Martha takes off her sandals, her toes curling into the hot sand. She can feel the heat warming her up, travelling through her body, opening doors in her heart that have been locked up for so long. She walks slowly to a spacious area and drops her bag onto the beach.

Then she looks round, across the beautiful water, all across the deserted golden shore, across the dusty road where some old dilapidated barracks glow in the sunlight. Martha feels an unease, the empty windows staring back at her as if daring her to think rude thoughts about their dejected state.

"Where did *that* feeling come from?" Martha mutters. "I don't really like those barracks behind my back. It feels as if the door frames and gaping windows are peeking at me…"

Her toes wriggle in the hot sand, because if she keeps them still, the heat becomes too much! All is quiet; not even the cicadas chirp at her. All Martha can hear are the waves spluttering, muttering, hissing and sucking at the stones as if trying to cling on to the golden beach a bit longer. She walks to the sea and gingerly dips her one foot into the clear water. "It's so warm," she gasps, moving her foot from side to side, "and so clear, and pure…" She spins round, suddenly excited, almost desperate to get into the water, to feel it, to experience its freedom.

Martha looks round before tugging her dress off, then looks round again in all directions before folding it up and putting it with her bag and sandals. Another searching look – and then she removes her watch and necklace. Her head keeps swivelling left to right, right to left. Each time her eyes pass the old white barracks they slow down, they search, checking the dark windows, the half broken door frames… Martha still hesitates, struggling to turn her back on the road and barracks, worried that as soon as she is in the water some tourists will come along and she'll be trapped… Nothing stirs though, nothing at all, and suddenly Martha takes a deep breath and marches with determined steps to the water. She keeps walking until the water comes to her waist, revelling in its comfortable warmth.

Martha sighs with pleasure – then shrieks as something bites her! She looks down in panic, shaking her leg away from whatever it was! There she sees the little fish swimming around her, and her newly found giggle comes out, bouncing along the waves. "Those fish! Well, at least I can advise people based on experience now, rather than rely on my holiday rep information!" Each time a fish nibbles her, she has to suppress a small scream, as it catches her by surprise, and for a split second the sensation brings bad memories, but Martha is determined to learn to accept the fish and to become used to them.

"I'm a victor!" – her odd giggle again – "I'm an overcomer, for I have overcome the fear those fish bring up!"

She cringes a little, as she can hear her counsellor reminding her to not ever make light of her past experiences. "Is that what it is?" she wonders. "I'm not really making light of them, am I? It's just those fish, and…" She stops, suddenly tired of thinking everything through, or analysing her thoughts and feelings. The warm sand, the smooth feel of the sea, soothes her soul as well as her muscles; and floating on her back, Martha smiles up at the blue sky, with the white golden glowing sun staring down on her, and whispers, "Thank you, Pastor Volodya. I'm being gently led at the moment, I think!"

10

MARTHA STAYS ON THE BEACH AS LONG AS SHE can but feels herself getting more agitated the nearer lunchtime comes. "I will be late, and to rush in this heat..." she says, then looks at her shoulders and groans, "I will need to get out of the sun anyway. Not even factor fifty copes with this sun!" She touches her shoulder gently, relieved that her skin doesn't feel tight... yet! She struggles with her dress, her body still a little damp, and tries to ignore her disappointment at having to leave this beautiful piece of Crete! "After lunch I'm busy," she says, then remembers the skin on her shoulders and rolls her eyes. "No more today, anyway."

Martha quickly looks in her notebook. "I can do tomorrow morning," she smiles, and looking back at the water, adds, "I'll bring my pencils! I know the sand and salty air might not be the best for them – but look at those colours!" For a moment she can see Anna's paintings and she understands her new friend a bit better. "Those colours do invite you to add the movement, the energy and the blending of colours," she says, staring at the play of water and sand, forgetting about lunch.

Her stomach suddenly makes a noise, making Martha jump, the noise too sudden for her liking! "Lunchtime, and I still need to get back to the resort! Tomorrow I will come back." She slips into her sandals and walks up onto the dusty road again, gasping a little at the heat wafting off the surface. She tries to rush but gives up on that idea after just a few yards. The heat is making her gasp, the hot air hurting her lips, steaming up her glasses, and Martha slows down, wishing that she had more water with her.

The following morning Martha feels a little better prepared, and carefully adds pencils and paper to her beach bag. More drinking water too, for yesterday morning her small bottle didn't last very long!

Locking her door, she looks round the resort, suddenly worried. "I hope I did all my tasks? I love that deserted beach so much, it can easily take over my thinking." She gets her Lifeline out and double-checks her schedule. Nothing is listed, and her programme makes it clear that this is her own time. She is relieved, but after a moment, quickly scribbles down, "Don't let the beach take over."

She pulls a face, hearing the Voice in the distance explaining to visitors how "Martha gets very obsessed, and will forget to eat and sleep, which led to her weight loss". Martha can feel her cheeks burning even now, remembering the visitors' looks. It made her feel weak, incapable, like some mad artist who just lived for her artwork, unable to take care of herself, let alone take care of others. She could sense their sympathy for her husband – poor man, fancy having a wife like that... Of course, the posh Voice had told her numerous times that to have more weight than necessary was not just a health risk, it also showed poor self-discipline and a lack of understanding of stewardship. Martha had dreaded the mealtimes, and at first would find snacks when by herself, unable to eat under his staring gaze, accompanied by statistics and warnings. But he always found out when she had been in the kitchen behind his back, and she hadn't dared in the end, and also had come to accept her new normal. Even now, after all this time, she knows that food is not an easy area for her...

How did I get there? Martha thinks, wondering how she went from checking her schedule to asking questions about food and the quantities of it...

The beach is deserted as ever, and Martha scans the entire area again, just to make sure. The colours are just as vibrant, and she pulls out her towel and sets herself up close to the water. First, she just looks, her eyes noting all the details: the tiny coloured flecks in the sand, the smooth pebbles, the curling white fingers of each wave, the blue sky reflected in the stunning blue water... She smells the salty air, filled with new quantities of salt each time a wave rolls over itself. The heat off the golden sand brings its own smell, and her toes dig into the hot grains, bringing that relaxing sensation again. After a very long time of soaking up the smells, the sounds, the warmth, Martha pulls out her paper and pencils. She looks at them and wishes that she had more blue!

"Maybe tomorrow I should go to Iraklion again," she says, the hot bus journey, the noisy city all in stark contrast to the quiet, peaceful beach... "I do need more blue," she argues with herself, "so it will be worth it in the end." For a moment she wonders if Anna could get them for her, bring them along or something... "Sunday is still a long way off, and I don't know if she can afford those pencils – and I don't want to put her in a difficult position," she thinks, knowing how expensive each individual pencil is. Then all Martha can think of are the soft lines of the frothy waves; the grey, scrubbed pebbles with occasionally a dark line on them; the golden sand that is only golden from further away... Martha seems lost to the world, but every now and then she looks round, checking the area, looking along the dusty road both ways, listening, squinting against the glare...

Just before lunchtime she spots the tiny speck next to Dia, clearly another tiny island, hardly visible in the heat haze. Martha looks across the water at the various colours on Dia, now a little blurred because of the heat, and sighs. "I could find so many things to draw," she says, feeling a familiar urgency come over her. It makes her smile, and she wonders whether she should write it in her Lifeline, as it would be a point for her journal: "Felt great need to draw things, all sort of things. Felt my mind starting on a list, prioritising various scenes." Martha chortles, imagining another part of her heart receiving a light colour, replacing another dull grey area with life and light.

"How I have missed my drawing," Martha says, her finger very lightly tracing the grey pebble on her paper, the shading making it look washed, sun-kissed and polished. She feels a little thrill, as she always used to do when enjoying her art. The feeling is so new, and it still has dark edges to it, fear swirling, blending the edges like its own heat haze. The sweet sense of achievement replaces another splinter of darkness in her heart, and Martha, for the very first time in forever, can spot a tiny glimpse of light at the end of her tunnel, and allows herself for just a few moments to wonder if there is healing for her heart and mind after all.

That evening she writes again in her sister's gaudy notebook, describing the water, the hot sand, the feel of her pencils... her need for more colours.

It is almost dark, but the air is still warm, and Martha doesn't feel the rush to go to bed before a certain time this evening. "Maybe I am getting there," she whispers, "although I can't imagine being whole again. Not now, not ever. Just to feel relaxed though, and happy..." She can recollect the moments on the beach, how the warmth from the hot sand made her whole body feel calm, how the endless chattering waves soothed her. "Then I end up writing down in my Lifeline that I need blue pencils, otherwise I will just forget. My memory is all over the place, and I know the counsellor has explained it all, but still..."

She looked through her counselling notes earlier this evening, wondering if there had been any messages of hope before. None of her counselling notes held the slightest glimmer of light; instead they added to the darkness of her tunnel: things Martha had taken for granted, words she had believed, incidents she thought she had experienced... It had turned out to be based on lies, mirages, clever manipulation... This evening she could see how her despair had grown along with the notes, and she vaguely remembered some of the sessions – remembered her fear, her frustrations, her unbelief, her anger... Anger that was usually directed at the wrong people, like her sister and brother-in-law, or the counsellor. It had been a time of hurt and confusion, and dark day had followed darker night, until she slowly managed to find some sort of balance again. By the time she had applied for holiday rep, the darkness in her heart had been replaced by a dull grey – cold and clinging to the furthest corners of her heart, like an autumn mist in the Cotswolds.

Looking out over the dark water Martha feels sadness rather than anger. Over time she has come to realise that so much of what the counsellor told her was true. Her joy and peace when drawing has brought more light and has helped her to accept some of what her counselling notes told her this evening. With the acceptance comes hope, for it will put some of the lies straight, and gives Martha a chance to undo some of the damage. "Drawing helps, and of course, none of my pencils has been sharpened down; I have always been fully aware of what I'm doing when sharpening them!" She sighs, as it puts another piece in its rightful place; another step towards completing the very dark puzzle. It also uncovers another grey part, leaving a soft, coloured patch in its place.

Her gaze drifts over Dia, then comes to a full stop at a little flicker of light on the island. The light disappears, then reappears half an inch to the right, burning steadily for a few moments, then disappears altogether. Martha breathes out, having held her breath inadvertently. *A light on Dia island? Or was it just a little boat passing by it? A boat should be visible from here, surely. It isn't very late – not really – but it has been dark for a little while, so who would be out at this time?* She keeps peering into the dark, but no more light can be seen. *Maybe Dimitris, or one of his friends, busy entertaining tourists on their boat? Maybe they allow people to camp on Dia island, or they have ranger-type people who check on the animals? It's so quiet...*

Martha decides to call it a night, determined to get more blue pencils in the morning, as well as some red, as she realises that she needs more colours for the sand and the pebbles! "It's so beautiful, so wonderfully made," she says, her mind imagining the shading needed for the sand, made up of so many different-coloured specks!

11

MARTHA'S MORNING STARTS THE USUAL WAY, but straight after breakfast she meets the young couple that wanted to walk the Gorge. "Did you enjoy it?" she asks them, smiling, still feeling a little envious of their confidence and the way they hold hands.

They nod, first smiling at each other, then at her, and the woman says, "Yes, thanks! The book was right though; I was just exhausted by the time we got back to the hotel!" She giggles, and the young man next to her actually blushes.

Martha feels a little uncomfortable, wondering what the joke is. Are they laughing at her? Did the information she gave them misinform them?

"He almost passed out, you see," the woman laughs. "It was so very hot, although incredibly beautiful. You should see the photos we took!"

Martha's eyes light up, and the woman promptly pulls out her phone, and after a few quick flicks shows the screen. Martha gasps. The pictures are just stunning: rough rocks covered in soft green bushes, blue sky overhead...

The last one is of the beach. "That's the end bit," the woman explains. "We were just baking hot and sweaty, so we were thrilled to see the beach! Well, mister here" –

she laughs again, and the young man joins her, in an embarrassed way – "mister here ran up to the water, kicked his walking boots off, and ran straight in, fully dressed!" Martha stares at the young man, not sure if she should laugh, or whether he will think her rude… The couple are in fits of laughter by now, so Martha allows herself a chuckle, smiling as pleasantly as she can, hoping that the young man won't think that she is laughing *at* him… "Well," the woman continues, "soon it was time for us to get back, and he was still wet… They gave him a bin bag to sit on and were muttering and tutting. The driver almost refused to let him on the bus!"

Martha feels the shock all the way through her body at these words! Her mind starts at various options and possibilities, scrambling for solutions. "What would you have done if they had refused you?" she asks. The idea of being stuck on the south coast without any transport, nowhere to stay the night – well, the whole idea is enough to make her shoulders tight and her pulse rise!

The couple just laugh, as if they can't see a problem at all, and they assure her that they would have found a way round it all.

Martha looks at them, incredulous. "Surely, that was the last bus back, so you would have been stuck?" she says.

The couple shrug, and the man explains that they had her number, so they would have just given her a call and asked her to sort it out with the bus driver, or for her to arrange a taxi, or something like that.

"Glad you managed to get on the bus," Martha says, doing her best to make her smile seem genuine, feeling her hands starting to shake.

What would she have done had the couple called her? Argue with the bus driver? *This couple is so confident and sure of themselves. If they couldn't persuade the driver, no way would I have prevailed... It would have been a disaster. And organise a taxi? How? I wouldn't even know where to start!*

"Those photos look amazing though, and I'm really pleased you had such a good day. I'm not surprised you were tired; it does look like hard work!"

The woman nods and admits that the next day she was more tired than she had expected and that it was mainly the heat.

Martha agrees, "I know what you mean. Even a short walk drains you, just because of the hot air and dust!"

Soon she experiences her own words on her way to the bus stop. The road seems hotter and longer than last time, but at least the bus has little curtains to shade out the sun.

Iraklion is noisy and busy as usual, but Martha is pleased to find herself coping with it. "No sitting down on that little bench, shaking," she says to herself, feeling pleased. "Now for the little streets. At least it's quiet there!" Walking into Anna's shop is a relief, and again Martha feels proud of how far she has come. Anna looks up when Martha walks in, and her smile is warm and kind as usual.

"Hi, Anna," Martha says, smiling back. "I need more colours! I just bought the pencils to draw Dia, as I really wasn't sure about drawing again. It's been so wonderful though, and now I've started on the water's edge, and I need more blue, and some warmer colours as well!"

Anna looks very pleased, and together they walk over to the different pencils. Martha can feel a little thrill. Last time she was so hesitant and really only bought a few pencils, not even sure that she would dare to use them! This time it's different, for she knows she will use them! She has found herself pulled in, soothed, calmed by her drawing, as well as experiencing the excitement of drawing what she sees.

"Looking at the water, the sand, the stones, I actually felt like drawing the way you do it; it's such a wonderful way of looking at the scene!"

Anna laughs and explains that she really can't do realistic art but loves how colours combine and give movement and an impression.

"I love your paintings," Martha says, smiling, "and I think it's incredible how you make the colours show the energy and feel of the place! I wouldn't know how to get that across. I like drawing whatever I see, but I can't actually make it up; I'm very limited!"

Anna shakes her head. "To draw real pictures with coloured pencil, that is what I call a gift! I can't get a line straight; I'm hopeless! I suppose we always feel that about other people's work!"

Martha nods, then they both turn back to the pencils, Martha softly fingering them.

"Here are the blue ones. Do you know which ones you will need?"

Anna looks at the different shades of blue and Martha shrugs, trying to remember what she has bought already! She pulls her Lifeline out and turns the pages, looking for the colours she bought. She can see her fingers trembling, feeling embarrassed to show Anna how dependant she is on her notebook, not even able to remember what she bought about a week ago, needing lists to get her through her day, otherwise she can't even remember what her own job is called...

Instead, Anna says, "What a good idea! I keep forgetting which colours I got, what brushes I used last time, and where I got the paper or canvas from! Every time, I need to start searching and trying things out again, whereas if I made a note, I'd be alright! Thanks, I will use this!"

Anna looks so pleased that Martha can feel herself relaxing. The shaking stops and she smiles at Anna, her eyes only a tiny bit blurry. "My memory is really, really bad. I need to make lists and everything just to get through the day," she admits – another first. She has never before admitted voluntarily that her memory is terrible and that she can't cope with life without her Lifeline! This feels just right though, although Martha doesn't explain why her memory is this bad. "It does help though, and you're right, I should have always used it for my drawing, as it does save a lot of time. Once I had pencils that were just awful. They were advertised as soft but turned out to be rock hard. I gave them to the kids' club in church," she laughs. "I almost bought them again next time I needed pencils, but somehow I recognised the box and didn't. I wasn't sure, but later I saw them in the church and remembered then..." Martha also remembers her beautiful pencil set, the best ones she ever had. She can still feel the joy when using them, but this is all overshadowed by the horror she felt that day when she opened the box to find them all sharpened down to about an inch and a half...

Martha shakes herself, forcing the Voice and all the images from that day to retreat, focussing herself on the blue pencils instead. "Pacific blue, of course; denim is nice too. Maybe aquamarine? Midnight blue will be good as well, and indigo. These will mix well with the greens I have!"

Anna nods, holding out a small paper bag.

"Now for some red – probably this one, mahogany; it's nice and dark. Razzmatazz – that sounds great," Martha laughs, putting the pink shade pencil in the bag. "I'll have mango tango as well. It's a great orangey shade; it will mix well."

Anna agrees. "Yes, you just need a few colours and the mixing options are amazing! Hard to get the same shade again afterwards though!"

Martha grins, and explains that with pencil it's a little easier.

"Of course, I hadn't thought about that!" Anna says, walking slowly to the till.

Martha pays, and then mentions the light over at Dia. "I wonder if they have people staying overnight – like animal workers or something?" Anna's face has turned very serious and Martha feels herself becoming a little worried as well. "I only saw the light for a short time; maybe it was a boat at the side of the island... It was very dark out that way, so I can't be sure."

Anna shakes her head and says that there is no reason for anyone to go that way in the dark.

"Maybe a tourist boat coming back late?" Martha persists, unsure why she feels it's important to be a boat.

Anna explains that the tourist boats wouldn't go that close to the island in the dark, and not at that time, anyway.

The two women look at each other and Martha tries to laugh it off. "Well, maybe I just imagined it. I was really tired, and it was only there for a few seconds."

Anna nods, and says that she will mention it to Dimitris. "We will pick you up on Sunday again?" she asks, giving the statement the intonation of a question.

Martha nods, finding herself looking forward to Sunday.

"Do text me if you see the lights again, alright? It might not be anything. Like you say, it might be someone checking on the animals. There are Kri-Kri on Dia, and there might have been some sort of accident – who knows? Anyway, Dimitris can think about it." She suddenly smiles again, and Martha feels relieved. The tense situation made her feel tense as well!

Martha tries to tell herself to follow Anna's lead and leave it with Dimitris. She has to keep reminding herself that it is nothing to do with her; it's not her responsibility at all. She has enough to keep her head busy – but thinking about thieves and lights feels safer and more comfortable.

Soon Martha finds herself back at the busy bus station, pleased with her successful shopping expedition. Then she realises how pathetic that is, to see buying pencils as a major obstacle. Her heart sinks a little when looking round at other people. "They won't think twice about going to town," she sighs, "and to me a shopping trip without a panic attack counts as a huge victory. I suppose it's better than last time, but I still have such a long way to go."

12

MARTHA SITS ON HER BALCONY, 'BLESSING journal' on the table, as well as her gaudy-coloured notebook. She sighs, looking out over the dark blue water, the sun having gone to bed already.

In her journal it says, "Went to Iraklion again, to get more pencils. No panic attack." Tears steam up her glasses. "How feeble," she says, her voice bitter, mouth drooping. "What sort of entry is that? How can that be a blessing? I'm so tired of being weak, Lord!" She looks at the line before describing her shopping trip. "Mr and Mrs Thomas trusted me enough to sort out their problems if things had gone wrong." *The very cheerful and over-confident Mr and Mrs Thomas, that is. The young couple who just seem to smile at each other a lot, and who have no problem with long, tiring days, and who happily took on the Cretan bus driver who initially refused to let Mr Thomas onto the bus as he was soaking. If their confidence and strong character hadn't been able to change the bus driver's mind, they would have called me to sort it out...*

Martha stares at the thin roof over her balcony, to stop the tears from running down her cheeks. "What would I have done? Lord, they would all have known how totally incompetent I am! How could I ever argue with a bus driver, forcing him to take a wet tourist on board? Where would I find a taxi to get them?" Her shoulders cramp together, and the shakes start. She can just imagine it: Mrs Thomas' cheerful voice ringing her on the rep phone, telling her how the bus driver won't let her husband on the bus because he's wet. Martha, using a very calm holiday rep voice, would ask, "What happened exactly? I see. Well, let me speak to the driver and we'll have this sorted in a moment!" But she wouldn't say that, would she?

Martha's breathing is coming faster and faster, growing more and more desperate by the second. "I wouldn't even know where to start! Would I really ask for the driver? Surely, he's not going to listen to some woman on a phone? So I would need to call a taxi company, but who would pay?" Martha can just imagine the couple wormed between rocks to stay out of the cool night air, huddled together for extra warmth, suffering with severe hypothermia, or maybe even dead?

"After all, they've just had a gruelling walk, and must be exhausted. He is soaking wet as well, which won't improve matters. When the taxi driver can't find them, he will contact me again, won't he? Or will he just shrug and leave it? Will the hotel ask me when they don't appear for meals? Or will people find them in the morning? I will have to inform headquarters – and what will I tell them?" Martha just makes it to the bathroom in time...

Once her body gets rid of what feels like every single food molecule, she sinks on the cool floor, her entire body still shaking, her head spinning. Somehow, she keeps wondering, "Who will I ring and what will I say?" Frantically, she tries to run through all the paperwork she has been given, wondering if there is anything about who to call in an emergency situation, her memory coming up with a blank.

Darkness closes in, and Martha struggles to breathe, struggles to stay fully conscious too. Her head lowers onto the cool tiles, and the coolness actually revives her a little. In the end, after what feels like an endless struggle to catch her breath, she manages to drag herself over to the balcony and takes hold of her Lifeline. She needs to find the number to report what has happened to the couple.

Turning to a page near the end of her notebook she spots this morning's entry: "Mr and Mrs Thomas managed to get back on the bus. Trip was very tiring. Note: even for fit people it's a hard thing to do."

Martha sinks back down on the balcony floor, staring at the words. "Mr and Mrs Thomas got back? Wait, surely the taxi driver found them huddled between some rocks, dead or half-dead? Aren't I supposed to report their death to a manager?" She feels confusion flooding her mind, doing nothing to improve her stomach. Very carefully she re-reads the entry. "Yes, they definitely came back." She closes her eyes, digging through various memories, pieces of memory, and images that could be memories. She travels back through the day: Iraklion, Anna, the bus, the young couple! She vaguely remembers speaking to them, and... "Of course, I saw her photos, we talked about the swim he had had, and how tired they had been the next day." Martha remembers talking about the beauty of the trip and how she wondered about the different colours! "So... they're not dead? I don't need to shout at a bus driver, or persuade a taxi driver to go and find them?"

Martha huddles up tight and sobs and sobs. She cries, and after a while realises that she's crying heartbreaking sobs not just because she thought a couple had died or she had to argue over buses, or anything else to do with Mr and Mrs Thomas. She also cries because of a reaction to her trip to Iraklion, the tension and fear she managed to control but which were obviously still there, affecting her. She sobs out of worry regarding that light on Dia and the unanswered questions linked to it. She even cries because of her pencils and drawings, the fear that she will lose it all again, and the idea that her enjoyment of her art is going to be short-lived. She weeps because of her weakness, her need to throw up whenever something scares her, her need to keep a Lifeline, her…

"Stop," she hisses, "just stop! I'm not a victim, I'm a victor. I can do all things through Christ who strengthens me!" She looks at herself, huddled tightly, chin on her bony knees, face wet with tears, and says out loud, "I'm an overcomer. I'm a victor. I can do all things through Christ, the Good Shepherd, who leads me gently, who carries me!" She takes off her soaking wet glasses and dries them. She tucks her hair behind her ear, dries her face and puts her glasses back on, all the time muttering, "I'm not a victim, I'm a…"

After a while she gets off the floor, picks up her pen and writes in the journal, "Had a panic attack afterwards, to make up for all the blessings. The blessing in the attack lies in the fact that I am becoming increasingly aware of the fact that I'm being carried and led gently. You can't rush sheep, and I can't rush my healing. Gentle improvements, small steps; the fact that I'm drawing again, the fact that I needed new pencils, the fact that I didn't collapse as soon as Mr and Mrs Thomas told me about their trip, and how they were going to get me to help – all that is progress. Gentle improvements, and I am grateful for each one."

She looks down at the words and feels a soft smile coming on, a calm inside replacing the terror of just a few moments ago. She pulls the gaudy notebook over and starts to write about the day. She remembers the photos, the fear upon hearing how they were going to call her if the driver wouldn't let them on the bus, her trip to Iraklion and the conversation with Anna. This makes her look up at Dia, but no light appears, and after a long time staring at the very dark black mass in the distance, Martha turns back to her notebook. She describes her panic attack but also writes how it ended and the insight it gave her, and how it has given her more patience with herself.

"It's hard to heal slowly," she writes. "I just want to be better. I just want to be like other people. I want to be confident too and smile and laugh. I want to move freely, just like others. I need to accept that it will take time. I need to accept small, gentle improvements. I need to count my blessings, like the fact that I can really smile, the fact that I'm drawing again, and that I have been in the sea…" That definitely brings out a smile, and she looks at the dark water, knowing that tomorrow she'll be able to go again. "Definitely at the top of blessings this month," she says. "My own private beach, without anybody seeing me in my swimsuit." She can't stop smiling, thinking about the golden beach, completely deserted, the little fish in the clear water, the sapphire blue waves…

That reminds her of sapphire ring warnings, and her smile shrinks, not quite turning into a frown though. "No thanks!" Martha says. "Not for me, not ever!" She tries to think of the beach without thinking of sapphires or rings, just beautiful hot sand, colourful smooth pebbles and warm water that happens to be blue. "Not necessarily sapphire blue," she says, thinking of the beautiful new pencils she has waiting. Martha looks at her thin fingers: not a ring in sight. Her fingers have been bare for a while now, but she still struggles with it. "I used to like rings, but I can't stand the sight of them anymore."

Martha can hear the Voice explaining to friends how she struggled with commitment and how a wedding ring made her feel constrained in their relationship... She can still feel the sinking feeling of utter shame, and it's only with difficulty that she forces herself to breathe in and out... and in and out... until she feels calmer. "I must be getting tired, to allow him into my memory like that," she mutters. She looks at the notebooks and journal, the dark sky, the even darker shape that is Dia island, and starts collecting her stuff.

Just before she goes into the little studio apartment, Martha turns and looks across one more time. That is when she spots the light again! She stops, feeling shock jolting through her, making her legs wobble, her shoulders cramping together straight away. "The light! It's back!" She walks inside, quickly drops the books on the little table, and dashes back out onto the balcony to see if she can spot the light again. It flashes a little further towards the side again, then disappears. "Just like last night!" Martha stares at the dark shape, hoping the light will reappear. Then she grabs her phone, and quickly bashes out a text to Anna – "Just saw the light again. Same place on the island. Xx" – and stands still, phone in hand.

"Right, actually, this is not my problem," she says, trying to convince herself, for the whole thing scares her. "I don't know why I'm feeling scared, for even if it is what Dimitris was talking about, it will be just some guy digging up ancient artefacts. He might be very gentle in normal life," she adds, imagining some archaeologist, thin face, glasses, little goatie... "Dimitris will know what to do, so that's that!"

13

MARTHA WAKES UP FEELING HUNGRY. NOT surprising, having lost her entire dinner last night! One of the first things she does is check her phone to see if Anna has replied. She has.

"I told Dimitris. He says he will check it out."

Martha sighs with relief. "Good, that's that done, then!"

Not many people come for information after breakfast, and soon Martha is back in her studio apartment to pack her beach bag. She carefully packs her pencils and paper, especially the paper where she has started the drawing of the water's edge. "I can do those lines on the pebbles now and mix the colours for the sand..." Her Lifeline gets packed, of course, and her factor fifty suntan cream. Martha can't believe it when she sees her hands shaking a little. "I'm getting so excited about the beach! Just the warm water, the hot sand, the peace, the beautiful colours everywhere..." She smiles to herself, and walking along the very hot and dusty road, catches herself humming.

Martha actually stops in the middle of the road and gasps. "I'm *humming!* I can't believe it. Lord, you've given me a song in my heart, after all these years! I truly can't remember the last time that I sang to myself – or

94

hummed." Her eyes go blurry, but these are tears of joy and gratitude. "It feels just so good, and my hope is growing, but the steps are so small, and progress is so slow," she says, thinking about last night's bathroom episode.

Soon Martha is on 'her' beach, as she has started to call it. After all, so far this beach has been deserted. She is worried though, wondering how long it will last. "It just seems too good to be true," she thinks, spreading out her towel, all the while scanning the area round about.

As usual her eyes check out the deserted barracks twice. "They give me the creeps," she mutters, brushing some sand off her knees. "It's the gaping holes, the dark windows, the fact that there are a few barracks close together. It just makes me constantly feel like someone is watching me!"

Once she is satisfied that nobody is nearby, she quickly gets into the warm water. Of course, she has established her own routine for her beach time. First a swim; then she dries up a little, which doesn't take long at all; then she gets her drawing stuff out and moves her towel closer to the water's edge to get the best view of the part she is drawing. After a while, usually when she feels her body can't keep up a steady temperature of just over thirty-seven degrees any longer but is fast approaching boiling point, she will put her art things away carefully, then have another dip. First, she will check the whole area again, of course, and after that second swim she will dry up, get dressed and walk back to the resort in time for lunch.

Martha looks at the blue water, revelling in its warmth, grinning at the little fish, gasping when a larger one nibbles, and thinks, "I never used to be this structured. I never organised things the same way all the time." It grieves her and makes her realise how much she has changed. "Should I change this one back? Should I really force myself to be spontaneous only, never doing things the same way twice?" Martha thinks about that for a bit. "On the other hand, always doing things in a novel way becomes a structure in itself! Anyway, lots of people like routine. I just cling to it more than others, I suppose. But then, I have changed things round a few times and I was fine!"

Martha has started to insist that she is getting better. "After all, I'm a victor. I get to make decisions. I have choices. I'm an overcomer..." She also manages to partly ban last evening's scene from her mind. She pulls a face. "Fine, it goes wrong sometimes, but I know I'm getting stronger!"

Soon she is dry enough to get her drawing out. She feels the thrill about the new pencils again, and starts on the pebble, her hair tucked behind her ear, glasses firmly pushed up. For a few seconds her hand shakes with excitement, and Martha has to take a few deep breaths to calm herself down. "I should have done this a long time ago, Lord, and I felt for so long that You had taken all joy, hope and peace away from my life. I blamed You, saw myself as victim who couldn't possibly find anything good, because of Your hand on me for evil." She has to look out over the sea for a bit, waiting for her eyes to dry in the hot sunshine. "How foolish I was, and how broken – and how I resented my sister's words, that You had thoughts of good towards me, and not of evil, to give me hope and a future. I felt my life was over and I just had to live out my days, but here I am! I have a job; I have my art again; I have hope – and I actually have hope for a future too. And I know that You will carry me and lead me gently along." She sniffs, her glasses steaming up again, and suddenly giggles. "Not much hope in finishing this drawing if I keep analysing my life and feelings!"

Martha forgets the time, what with her red, blues and greens mixing the colour perfectly, and the sand turning out exactly the right shades. Just when she adds the last little streak of blue to the edge of a wave, her stomach gives a loud protesting snort, making her clutch her tummy! She looks at her watch, and gasps.

"Not again! It's lunchtime, and there is no way I can rush along that hot and dusty road! I will be late, and they will all be staring at me! How do I ask for my lunch? Who do I go to, and what will they say? They might not even give me anything…" She can feel the panic starting, and tears burn again. "Just when I thought I was getting somewhere! Look at me now; late for lunch and I'm falling apart." She suddenly pictures the young couple, which doesn't help! "They were trapped on the south coast, having to argue with the bus driver, with the prospect of having to spend the night there and everything, and they were absolutely fine. It's not fair…"

This very petulant thought stops the panic, as even Martha realises that she's not in any danger. She carefully and quickly puts her things away, gets dressed in a great rush, and walks as fast as the heat allows her back to the resort. She looks behind her a few times, especially towards the barracks, as she always feels prying eyes watching her. She knows it's nonsense, but then, she didn't know about all her husband's cameras everywhere either, did she?

To Martha's relief lunch hasn't finished at all!

"I really made myself panic over nothing," she says to herself later in her apartment, "just like yesterday. Well, maybe it's a good sign that my panic attacks are now about things I worry about or imagine, rather than me panicking about real events!" This makes her wonder enough to write it down in her Lifeline, wanting to put it in her 'blessing journal' tonight, and to think about it today as well. "After all, I wasn't sick when the woman told me they'd planned to contact me if all else failed, but I had the panic attack when I thought they'd died and I would have to notify the manager and everything." Martha looks down at her Lifeline and suddenly adds, "I also worked this out logically, so I have some reasoning capacity evidently."

The Voice can be heard then, louder and louder, its posh accent making her shiver. "You can't think for toffee, woman," making toffee sound like 'toffay', as well as making the word 'woman' sound like the sort of word that requires green soap and water. "I really don't understand what makes you think arguing with me is appropriate. You have no idea how that makes me feel, and as you know how immersed I am in my work at the moment, I can only conclude that you are very selfish, although I've always denied that. I can't believe that I have defended you so many times towards my friends, and even my family!" She feels the mortification she felt then coursing through her immediately, but this time Martha recognises it for what it is.

"Stop," she says out loud. "Stop. I know your game. And don't pronounce 'toffee' like that," she suddenly adds, with bravado accompanied by a rather nervous giggle. Then she wonders, "What if I had been much stronger, and had confronted him, and seen through his behaviour and manipulation straight away? What would have happened then?" Guilt replaces the giggles, and Martha can feel it weighing her down. "I really should have seen it, shouldn't I?" she asks the painting in her apartment. "Maybe my clear-thinking skills weren't great after all. Then when it was pointed out to me, and when it was almost too late, I still didn't see it. My sister Louisa was so patient, I must have driven her mad!" Martha feels very grateful that Louisa was such a help; not only for physically saving her life, but also for helping her with her mental health – and is still supporting her now!

That reminds her... and she quickly pulls her drawing from her bag, places it on the table in a good light and carefully takes a photograph on her phone. Then she sends the picture to Louisa, and says, "My first drawing! Had to go to the city twice for pencils!"

She looks at the drawing, feeling herself relaxing, her shoulders feeling soft and free. "My first drawing since... since the pencil thing," she whispers, touching the coloured pebbles gingerly with one finger. A funny feeling starts under in her stomach, wriggling, churning, until it bursts out in a very subdued, quiet but excited shriek, and Martha actually has to waggle her hands along with it, suddenly feeling like an excited teenager! "My first drawing in ages, and I loved doing it! The feel of the pencil in my hand, the way the shapes come to life, the blending of colours..."

She takes another picture on her phone, then turns the drawing over and writes on the back, "To Anna, thank you for your kindness." She puts it ready to take on

Sunday, smiling a little, hoping that Anna will like it, worried all of a sudden; then remembering her soft, kind eyes, and somehow just knowing that she will like it. *She won't react like him*, she thinks, feeling the sharp edge of resentment; fighting against bitterness digging a way into her heart.

14

SUNDAY MORNING FINDS MARTHA UP EARLY and excited. She hesitates with her drawing in her hand. "Won't Anna think it weird that I'm giving her a drawing? I would like to thank her though, and I'm sure she'll understand." Martha frowns a little, pushing her glasses up, tucking her hair behind her ear, taking deep breaths… and soon she is ready to leave. She recognises the car and is amazed at how pleased she feels when seeing them come. "I'm feeling a sense of belonging, of community. It's my friends in that car; at least, that is how it feels like. I just hope…" Her thoughts trail off, as she suddenly remembers how bad she is at finding sensible friends. "After all, I couldn't even find a good husband! I didn't see the signs. I couldn't tell that he wasn't a Christian and that he was an evil man." But was he? Or was it right what he said all the time, calling her the most selfish woman he had ever met; calling her thick, calling her ugly, useless…? His reasons for calling her those words always sounded so logical, but her sister Louisa and her husband kept repeating that he had no right to call her any of that.

Martha sighs, then pulls the corners of her mouth up in a broad smile, for Dimitris' car has pulled up. *Those thoughts will have to wait – or even better, disappear for good!*

She gets into the car, greeting Anna and Dimitris, the warm, pleasant feeling returning, the Voice nowhere to be found. As soon as Martha is belted in and Dimitris has started the car, Anna turns round, her eyes bright. "How were the new colours? Were they right for what you wanted?"

Martha feels the thrill again – the thrill of talking with a friend about art, to mirror a friend's face, to both feel the deep joy after creating something beautiful. So she nods and explains that it was just what she needed, and a little shyly she hands the drawing to Anna, the written words on top.

Anna reads them and her eyes glow, her whole face alight. "Thank you," she says, then turns the paper over and gasps. "Oh wow! Martha! I... oh, this is amazing! I don't know what to say, I feel so honoured!" She goes quiet for a moment, intently studying the drawing.

Martha feels her shoulders tense up with each passing second, until Anna turns round again, her dark eyes luminous with tears.

"Martha, this is incredible! It is so, so beautiful! I... well, are you sure it's alright for me to have this? It's so wonderful!"

Martha's tensions leave her in a big rush, and she smiles a happy, relieved smile, nodding vigorously.

Anna nods in response, her tanned finger touching the paper almost reverently, her eyes full of admiration. "You really are an amazing artist, Martha," she says. "This drawing is just so beautiful, the colours perfect, and I have no idea how you did the sand! I can almost feel the grains, feel the heat, hear the waves... Thank you so much. I appreciate it very much – more than you can know – for I know what a drawing means."

Now it's Martha's turn to feel her eyes sting with retained tears.

Dimitris coughs, and says, "What about me? Nobody has said anything nice to me yet!"

The two young women laugh, but Martha feels a tiny sliver of fear creep in. *Does he mean that? Does he mean that we have been selfish, focussing on our own interests, even though we should be really grateful that he is taking the trouble to drive us to church?*

"I do appreciate you giving us a lift," she says, trying to make her voice sound warm and dripping with thankfulness, forcing the shakiness to stay out of it.

Dimitris' head comes up with a shock, and he looks at her in the mirror, his very dark eyes wide in surprise. "Martha! I was just joking. I love giving you both a lift, and it's not a chore at all! I'm going to church too, so what is better than to go with a few people together? I'm sorry; I shouldn't have teased you." His voice sounds genuinely sorry and Anna elbows him. "Yes, yes, yes, I know – 'How many times have I told you...' – but I do apologise, and I'll be extra good, Anna!" He grins at his sister, whose dark eyes have taken on a very naughty glint. She suggests that he proves how sorry he is... Dimitris laughs and pulls a face.

Martha stays quiet. Part of her feels like smiling at the interchange between brother and sister, part of her cringes in fear. What if Dimitris was not sorry at all but felt he had to act the part? Will he turn on Anna as soon as they are alone?

After a while Dimitris says, "How about we go out on my boat tomorrow? I only have four older women who want to see around Dia and Paximadi – maybe swim, maybe not – so it would be lovely to have you both there as well!"

Anna's face lights up and she turns round to Martha excitedly. "Would you be able to come? Please?" she says, and Martha nods; tomorrow she has a day off, as nothing seems to happen on a Monday! Anna turns back to Dimitris. "What time, and where? I will get Gloria to man the shop," she says, her whole face glowing.

Martha can feel excitement growing inside her as well; Anna obviously loves going out on the boat and... *But what about a swimsuit? Do I really have to go round in a swimsuit in front of others?* She can feel her hands turning icy cold and clammy at the thought.

"I'm not going in the water though," Anna says. "Too much to bring otherwise!"

Dimitris rolls his eyes at that, and brother and sister tease each other for a while, Anna calling his boat a washtub without decent washing facilities, he calling her spoilt and shaking his head at someone who grew up at the seaside making so much fuss over sea water and sand...

Martha hardly hears what they say, for her heart is bursting with relief. If Anna isn't going to go in the water, she has the absolutely perfect excuse not to either! She comes out of her deep thoughts just in time to hear Dimitris say, "Would you be able to make a sketch or drawing or something of my boat? I love my washtub" – he sends a mock glare towards his sister – "and I would love to have an arty picture of it!"

Martha blushes bright red, her hands shake, and with one finger she just manages to push her glasses higher up her nose. "I would love to do that," she says, "and I've really got back into drawing, so I'll bring my pencils tomorrow."

It's hard to describe how I feel, she thinks, looking at the streets of Iraklion. Somebody has asked her to draw something – like a commission... *I feel... nervous? Proud? Excited? Worried? All of these probably...* She smiles. *What if he doesn't like it? What if I get the proportions wrong, and what if...* She takes a very deep breath, fingering her locket. *Of course, I'm an overcomer,* she tells herself. *I'm not a victim, and a tiny bright-coloured part of my heart says that I'm an artist...* She shivers a little at such a daring statement, shutting her ears against the Voice mocking her art work, asking her if she'd drawn something in the dark or when drunk – knowing full well that she had never had a drop of alcohol since their wedding night... She swallows, somehow fighting against the overpowering smell of alcohol in the car, a smell that wasn't there a few seconds ago... "I'm a victor," she whispers to herself. "I will overcome, and I can do all things..."

Walking into the church she pushes images of boats, blue smooth water and sandy beaches out of her head, telling herself that they can wait till tomorrow. *Of course, I mustn't let my imagination run away, but use my senses.* She grins, revelling in the 'artist' role, and her inside shaking with excitement about her first commission since... *Well, since too long,* she decides.

Martha struggles in church. The sermon is hitting too close to home. Pastor Volodya has taken up the next chapter and shows how God tells His people not to be afraid. "Do not fear, for I am with you, I will strengthen and uphold you and help you. Though you search for your enemies, you will not find them." He looks round the congregation, and Martha feels like hiding.

"Fear not? Is Pastor Volodya serious? If he knew what my life has been like, he would surely see that I have every ground to fear," she mutters to herself. "Almost dying – isn't that a reason to fear?" She tucks her hair behind her ear, feeling the strands getting greasy already, and she is struggling against her tears.

Pastor Volodya says that being courageous means doing what is right, no matter what. Martha feels like pulling a face. *He has obviously no idea. Does he know what the "no matter what" can stand for? And what if you don't even know what is right or wrong anymore, or when the other person is so much stronger, more powerful and more influential than you? Or when that person has the approval of friends, relatives and the church, and they see you as mentally ill, unstable at least, and a burden on the poor husband... Should I have stood up to him? What would have happened?*

But what if the pastor is right, and all my problems have come from my weak faith and giving in to fears and doubts? Would everything have worked out differently if I had obeyed and shown courage? Maybe I was selfish after all, wanting a life of ease and to go with the flow, rather than to stand up to my husband and trust God with the outcome... Maybe he would have changed and been convicted by my godly example, instead of grown worse and worse... Maybe my lack of courage made him worse, and maybe the difficulties were all from God, to prompt

106

me to trust Him and have faith in Him... Instead I withdrew more and more, too scared to face my husband, too scared to even recognise there was a problem – instead believing him, even when he almost killed me. What sort of faith was that? I obviously obeyed men more than God, so no wonder God left me to it!

The shakes start, and Martha fights against it as much as possible, tears steaming up her glasses, her head bent to hide her weakness. She feels a cool hand on hers – Anna's!

"It's alright," Anna whispers, "listen to the next few words; it's alright!"

Anna is right, and Martha somehow manages to hear Pastor Volodya's voice over the rushing sound in her ears. "This courage doesn't come from ourselves, of course. We are fallible human beings, given to fears and worries. It's the Lord that says, 'Be courageous, for I am with you.'"

Martha finds the noise in her ears has stopped, and so have the shakes.

"You see, we often think we have to rise to the occasion, to prove to God what a good choice He has made in calling us to be His follower," Pastor Volodya says, "and we forget that we are saved by grace. With this saving faith comes the strength to follow Him."

Martha sighs. *Yes, well, I haven't seen much strength, to be honest! If only I had been stronger a long time ago...* She feels herself calming down with each moment though, peace coming in as Pastor Volodya's voice carries on, knowing she will have to have a very good think about all this!

15

MARTHA HASN'T THOUGHT MUCH ABOUT PAS-
tor Volodya's words, but rather about Dimitris and his
boat. "It's just that I don't want to disappoint him with
the drawing," she says, tilting her chin whilst packing her
bag for the following day. "Paper, pencils, Lifeline, towel
for in case..." She smiles, feeling the relief again when
thinking how she got out of the whole swimming
dilemma... "Thanks, Anna," she says, then looks around,
slightly embarrassed by her own voice. "Now, what about
food? I told the staff that I won't be there for lunch
tomorrow, but do I need to bring some on the boat?
Dimitris didn't say anything. Maybe he wants to see me
stuck..." The thought comes out before she has a chance
to filter it. "Of course not; he's not like that!"

Martha sits down on her bed, staring at her sandals.
Would Dimitris really be different? After all, she only
found out about William by the time they were married.
Nobody believed her, only her sister Louisa and her
husband. In a sense she didn't even believe it herself...

"I'm very sure that Dimitris wouldn't keep quiet about
lunch just to see me suffer," she sighs, then mumbles,
"That was a silly comment to make," her toes in her
slippers wriggling their agreement. "I will need my sun
lotion stuff; a hat as well. Sitting on a boat in this heat

could be interesting. Maybe I will regret not bringing my swimsuit..." She pulls a face, knowing that she will not regret it, however hot she might get!

Straight after breakfast that Monday morning, Dimitris' old car is waiting for her, and Anna is driving! Martha gets into the passenger seat, a little hesitant – she doesn't like changes or surprises.

Anna smiles as she gets in. "Morning, Martha! I'm glad you're coming today. It will be lovely out on the water. The islands are gorgeous too; some of the colours out there are amazing."

Martha smiles. Yes, she's actually looking forward to it; she just hopes nothing too far out of her comfort zone will happen. The idea of going on a stranger's boat – well, *relatively* a stranger – is enough to bring on the shakes! Her fingers close around her golden locket, its warmth comforting.

Anna is quiet for a few moments, then in a softer voice asks, "I hope you're alright? You looked a little upset yesterday."

Martha nods and sighs. She knew Anna noticed how upset she was in the service, and even afterwards, although she felt better by then, she was still very thoughtful, mulling over Pastor Volodya's words.

"Are you alright now?" Anna repeats, looking at Martha, her eyes kind and soft.

Martha shrugs a little and admits that she really needs to think about the words carefully.

Anna agrees. "Yes, often Pastor Volodya's sermons take time to sort out in your mind," she says, starting the car. "Well, I'm really looking forward to this trip! I'm glad Dimitris asked us!"

Martha smiles, feeling a little thrill. She pats her bag. "I brought my pencils and paper," she says. "I'm actually looking forward to drawing today! I might have to take some pictures on my phone if I can't finish it before going back. I prefer to look at the real thing though; pictures always change the colour and the light."

Martha is worried about lunch, and she is aware that she is sounding a little nervous. Should she ask Anna? Or will Anna think she is accusing Dimitris of spitefulness? In the end she says, "I didn't bring any lunch, but maybe I can get some?" She pushes up her glasses, her hands sweaty. *Well, so much for showing courage! A simple question and I'm almost falling apart. How could I ever have stood up against William? Surely, You didn't expect me to, Lord? Surely, I did the right thing by giving in and going along with his moods...*

The silence in her heart is rather uncomfortable and her shoulders tighten up. Martha feels a subtle shaking inside which she knows will grow with each passing second. Then a calming hand on her arm brings her back, and Anna glances at her quickly.

"Are you alright? Don't worry about lunch. Dimitris has lots! Normally Andreas sorts out food, but he has the day off because Dimitris said we would be there."

Martha looks worried. *Is Dimitris expecting me to help steer the boat, handle ropes or whatever else needs doing on a boat?*

Anna chuckles; she obviously felt Martha's arm stiffen. "I have been with my brother many times. I'm probably a better sailor," she laughs. "Dimitris is too careful; I like sailing fast..."

Martha feels relieved, taking a deep breath, to clear her lungs more than anything.

"Anyway," Anna carries on, "Dimitris is always worried there might not be enough food. So now there is lots!"

Martha chuckles, thinking about her brother-in-law who loves his food and struggles to estimate how much is needed... She tells Anna and they laugh together.

"Well, in this case we are well off," Anna smiles. "There will a barbeque and there are salads and breads to go with it."

Martha can feel her stomach churning to show its approval!

Soon they drive into a harbour area, and Anna parks the car. Martha gets out a little slower and follows her to the boat. "It's lovely," she gasps. "I love the colours – and the shape!" The boat isn't very large but has been painted in cheerful colours and has two sheets strung over the top to make shaded areas. The two women get on board, and Dimitris looks up.

"Hi, Martha," he smiles, then turns to Anna. "Thanks for helping. Was the car alright?"

Martha grins to herself, recognising the tone... Anna punches her brother's arm and the two laugh, leaving Martha feeling more relaxed than she has been so far today. Anna goes to help Dimitris, looking very competent, after she has shown Martha a good place to set up.

"The older ladies will be better off sitting there," she points, "but if you sit here, you'll have a good view."

Martha nods, suddenly eager to get her pencils out, for the bright colours and interesting shape of the boat have made her want to draw! Soon she is busy drawing the faint outlines of the boat, trying to gauge how much is above the blue waves. The four ladies arrive, but she just nods and smiles at them, and soon all is ready!

The trip is wonderful. Martha forgets to draw every now and again, and somehow forgets how hard she finds it to draw from a picture... The shades are just amazing! They land on Dia island, and after wriggling just their toes in the water for a while, they walk up a path to where the barbeque area is. Dimitris has beaten them to it and just looks up, pointing with his head to where they should set up the salads and bread.

Martha shudders. "I don't envy Dimitris – having to barbeque in this weather!"

Anna giggles, looking at her very tanned brother, and then explains that in July and August it really is a lot warmer!

Martha pulls a face. "No wonder he is so tanned! Even I might tan in that sort of setting!"

They laugh, and soon lunch is on the way. The feta salad, white crusty bread and roasted pork steaks can be washed down with lemonade or wine. One of the older ladies wants wine, the rest just ask for lemonade and water. Martha finds herself staring at Dimitris, wondering if he will drink a lot of wine as well. He has none, just lemonade and bottled water, making her feel better. "Maybe he drinks it in the cabin though," she mutters to herself, then stops with a tiny gasp. *There I go again! Have I always been like this?* That makes her think. *I still blame William for who I am today. Surely, I should start facing my troubles and weaknesses?* The thought of doing so makes her feel very queasy, and she struggles with the last bit of bread. *Not today,* she thinks, then admits, *I should really show more courage. I know I was in danger, so maybe I had an excuse then. That excuse is now gone, so I should learn to trust God more. I should learn to rely on Him and draw my strength from Him.*

She knows why she hesitates to do so, and why blaming William feels better. *I'm afraid. That's all. I felt like God had left me, God didn't answer my prayers for protection, and didn't make me the wife William wanted. Now I'm not sure that He will give me enough strength to deal with all my fears and panic attacks.* She looks around – the sea just below them, blue as ever, Paximadi just a bit further away – and sighs. "Surely a God who made all this has the power to keep me."

Martha is shocked when Anna agrees, not realising she had spoken the words out loud! She turns to Anna and explains. "You know, when Pastor Volodya said about being courageous yesterday, I just really struggled. So many things have happened where I wasn't courageous at all. Even now, I'm afraid of so many things, and I can't see myself being brave ever!"

Dimitris listens as well, and he is the one that answers. "Sometimes it's taking tiny steps at a time. Sometimes it's looking back and seeing that actually we have grown. It's not always the obvious fight, the clear stand for justice in a public way. Sometimes it's getting up each day, knowing that it will be hard." He and Anna look very serious, and it has gone very quiet. Anna nods, her eyes filled with tears. "Our father was killed by robbers, killed on his boat. They were diving for ancient stuff and he surprised them. They entered the ship and killed him."

Martha is stunned, and just sits there staring at Dimitris. No wonder they had been so upset about the thieves! It wasn't the fact someone was walking off with Ancient Cretan things; it was the danger these thieves brought. So much for her kind man with the goatie...

"After that, my mother struggled in the mornings, and during the day. That is when we got to know Pastor Volodya. One of my German friends went to his church, then he invited me and we started going to the church as well. Which is why our English is so amazing," he grins suddenly, breaking the heavy spell that seemed to have landed on them all.

Martha giggles. She wouldn't dare to say anything to that!

"You see, that's what we learned about courage, to know what is right and do it. Even if it's small steps. It's hard, we know it is..." He looks at Anna, who nods, tears hanging off her eyelashes, ready to drop.

Martha is quiet, just very slowly nodding her head. "I see what you mean," she says. "I didn't think I would ever draw again... or go anywhere. These days here, though, I have come a long way. But there is still such a long way to go!" She knows that sounds a bit pathetic, but it's true.

Looking at some underwater amphorae later, just off the coast of the little island called Paximadi, Martha almost feels disappointed that she didn't bring her swimsuit. "Maybe swimming in front of others should be on my list of fears to conquer," she says, staring down in the dark blue water. Then she calls to Anna, "Those look beautiful," and Anna comes over.

Anna looks down too and nods. "Yes, you can look at them but they can't be touched. Dimitris thinks it's underwater stuff that is being stolen. Anything you dig up needs a certificate, otherwise it's worthless. You see, it needs documentation of provenance, papers to say where it's from, and what time period. Sometimes thieves use forgers who will produce documents. Then they will sell these artefacts on the black market. If you bring too much on the black market, it affects the real stuff. These people don't care though because in some places they will be paid a lot of money. They're often very ruthless, although some are just petty thieves. The ones that Dimitris' friend was talking about sound like the type doing it on a larger scale. I know he is worried about it."

Martha wonders if anybody knows how many amphorae there are in this spot, so they can be checked, but Anna shakes her head.

"No, there are so many! Once there is a storm, they often drift away a bit as well, so it's hard to tell. They won't take the obvious ones, of course."

Martha feels a little uneasy, glancing along the coast at the underwater caves, and all around, wondering if these men operate in the daytime as well...

16

MARTHA MANAGES TO FINISH THE DRAWING OF the boat, although it will need finishing touches.

Dimitris is impressed. "That really looks like my boat," he says. "I love the way you managed all the different colours!"

Martha blushes, pleased with his praise, unsure of how to react. Anna is impressed as well and explains that however nice the boat is, she loves the water and the way Martha has managed to draw the waves, making it look as if the boat is really moving through the sea.

It's quite late in the afternoon by the time they get back to the harbour. Martha feels tired, not just from the heat and from drawing the scene, but from the tension as well. She kept a lookout ever since Anna explained about the robbers.

"They don't usually work in the daytime," Dimitris explained at some point when he saw her looking around, "and we'll be back before it's dark. I told my friend about the light you saw on Dia, and he will get someone to check it out. It's probably nothing, but it could be a thief looking for artefacts. It will be hard to find them, as there are so many places where you can hide along this coast!" Martha nodded, thinking of the caves you can see and many large rocks where you could hide. She shivered a bit, looking at the islands, wondering if there might be a man sitting behind a rock, watching them through binoculars, wondering when they would leave. She was relieved when Dimitris started the engine and steered towards the coast again.

In the evening she struggles with her 'blessing journal' – not because she can't think of a single blessing but because she doesn't know where to start! "This was such a wonderful day, Lord. Thank You!"

She feels sadness for Dimitris and Anna. "Imagine losing your father like that," she whispers. Then she thinks of her own father. Her relationship with him is not great. He really admired her ex-husband – or rather his family and fortune... He saw William as an upstanding citizen, a pillar of the church and the local community. Even though she was almost killed by him, her father still seems to think it a pity that their marriage didn't work out. She has sensed that he blames her and feels she must have aggravated William somehow. "Which I probably did," she thinks aloud. "If I had been more courageous, more outspoken, more prepared to make a stand over matters, it might have worked out. Maybe he was just saying and doing all those things to see how far I would go." She stares at the black crocodile shape mass that is Dia. "He was probably annoyed by my tears and could see that I was weak and feeble. That made him do it more and more. He was right; I was selfish, just thinking of myself, and not realising how hard it must have been for him to have such a spineless wife." Tears fill her eyes and Martha lets them. "He always said it was all my fault, that I had come short as a wife, so he had to put up with everything." She can't see the island now, tears flowing too freely.

After a while Martha starts to calm down and certain incidents come to mind. "On the other hand, why did he have to destroy my pencils?" By now she is quite certain that she would never have sharpened her favourite pencils to death... He made her believe that she had and made all their friends and relatives think that she had – but she hadn't. This makes her dry her face, tuck her hair away and push her glasses up. "So maybe it wasn't all my fault?" She thinks back over her marriage and sees problems from the very first day. "The way he drank, and then pushed me and nudged me with his knee to make me fall over... Surely that isn't acceptable? The way he laughed at the church, and the people there, for believing him and for looking up to him..."

Martha leans back, feeling another corner of her heart receiving colour, replacing the dull grey. She had such a struggle believing her sister and the counsellor. Now, so much later, she is starting to see the truth of their words. She completely ignored her brother-in-law's words, for after all, as a policeman he was used to dealing with criminals. And her ex-husband wasn't a criminal, was he? He was just a man with a weak wife that exasperated him – a wife with no memory at all, who needed constant reminding of things. Like visitors...

Martha groans as she remembers the regular occurrence of visitors arriving without her expecting them. William knew, of course, and she could hear him explaining to them in rather loud whispers that his wife lived in her own world, absorbed with self... She had done her very best to save the day but had been shaking with distress and embarrassment. She remembers the counsellor's question, "Are you sure that he really told you?" She remembers her sharp answer, that of course he would have told her, probably numerous times, like he explained to her afterwards, and she had been too selfish to listen or take an interest, that was all. Now, though, Martha can feel doubt creeping in. Seeing that he lied on many other fronts, might that have been one of his cruel tricks? She just wonders...

The next morning, after seeing and helping a few couples, and welcoming new guests by giving them an overview, Martha feels exhausted. The night has been restless as she thought about how much of her marriage was based on lies. She manages to keep a happy smile for the guests though. Her jaw is aching more than ever, but she is determined to give clients the best service possible.

Another young, healthy-looking couple asks about walking the Gorge, and Martha hands them the leaflet with one hand while grasping her locket with her other. "It is very tiring, apparently," she says. "Another couple did it last week, and they told me how tired they were." She sighs, looking at them, the healthy couple smiling at each other with great confidence... Of course, she has to tell them how beautiful it is, and hesitates whether she should warn them about jumping in the sea fully dressed...

Once the last guest has gone, Martha collects the leftover brochures and rushes back to her apartment. It is almost lunchtime, and she is determined to have an early lunch and then head over to her private beach. She smiles, feeling the warm water already as she gets her bag together. She stops with her pencils in her hand, wondering about drawing something today. Yesterday's drawing of the boat was a bit of a marathon, leaving her hand and fingers tired. In the end she decides to take them, and some paper, just in case she sees something that really catches her eye. "Or I could draw those amphorae?" She thinks about the odd-shaped jars, their round handles sticking out like a monkey's ears, the bottom of the jar often pointed, so the bottle had to hang in a rack, presumably. The colour is a warm terra cotta though, and lying on the bottom of the sea, the blue-green waters swirling all around, large smooth rocks keeping the amphorae trapped... "I could do that dark-coloured one, like an amphora still life, I suppose." Her hand is still tired and sore, but she can feel her interest sparked to life and wonders what will prove stronger: her pain or her desire to draw?

The heat is incredible that afternoon. "I didn't realise this beach gets this much hotter in the afternoon!" Martha is soon in the water though, after her standard searching looks. This time she scans the water as well, and even stares hard at Dia and Paximadi in the distance. It's not just other people she is worried about, but what if there is an artefact thief nearby, waiting for dark? She knows that she isn't being very realistic, but she can't shake the image that Dimitris' words have painted in her mind when he told her about his father's murder.

The water is just perfect, apart from some of the larger fish nibbling her skin. The larger ones make her jump, as the nibbling almost feels like a bite! Martha loves lying in the bit where the waves froth and fight on the beach, enjoys the hot sunshine, the cool water hardly touching her, and then the cool wave comes chattering in, rushing over her, mumbling nonsense in her ears, before withdrawing with a disappointed whisper. Occasionally the little fish nibble her feet, making her squirm and giggle. Martha feels carefree, light and only a little sleepy! Last night was a big step, to allow herself to accept that she had been lied to and that William had twisted things round, not just *to* her, but also *about* her, painting an image of her that wasn't correct. Not once had Martha accepted that before, believing his words, believing the Voice pointing out her faults and mistakes.

Martha half dozes off on the water's edge, then decides to do some drawing after all. "Just a little outline of that amphora trapped by the grey rock," she decides. She gets comfortable on her towel, and once she is dry, starts working.

She squints at the picture on her phone, glad that she actually remembered it! "That's another first," she says, hearing the bitterness in her voice. "My memory seems to have been destroyed. I struggle to focus on tasks, but then yesterday I managed that drawing almost in one go! Maybe it does get better over time?" Seeing her Lifeline in her bag, she sighs, "I don't think I'll let go of that for now though! This morning I saw quite a few new people, although not as many as they will have in the summer, no doubt. I don't think I could cope in the summer."

This morning was enough of a struggle, as the manager turned up near the end, just as she handed the healthy-looking couple their leaflet about the Gorge. Martha still struggles every time she sees the manager; he is kind enough to her now, but the smell of alcohol on him is her undoing every time… Even this morning she felt her stomach turning and grunting in protest, her head feeling lighter by the second as well. She was very worried that she wouldn't make it to the end of the conversation, but somehow she did. "Courage, be courageous," she said to herself.

"At least it worked this morning," she smiles, "even though it never did before when I smelled alcohol! Another first... Lord, it's like I need to learn to live all over again!"

17

MARTHA ENJOYS THE AMPHORA. THE SHAPE IS not as easy to draw as it looks because the fact that it's underwater needs to show up as well. After a while she feels tired, puts her drawing materials away and just lies down to relax.

Martha lets the peace of the afternoon seep into her very bones. The heat is almost too much, but by lying very still, she can cope with it. She can hear cicadas in the distance, the occasional plane overhead on its way to Iraklion – but apart from that, just silence. Martha can feel herself drifting off, lazily wondering that if she falls asleep, will she wake up in time for dinner?

Just when she is almost gone, her ear registers a faraway noise. It's a noise she hasn't heard here before. Laughter, shrieks, shouts. For a moment Martha stays still. The noise is really very far away, so not important. Then she wonders, "What if it's coming this way? It must be moving, otherwise I would have heard it before!" She still hesitates, but another shout makes her open her eyes. She sighs, feeling way too sleepy and comfortable for this! In the end she sits up, nudging her glasses up on her nose, tucking hair that feels heavy with salt behind her ear. She looks round, trying to gauge where the noise comes from.

A long way off, along the coast, some people seem to be walking slowly along the road. Martha can't tell exactly how many, or what sort of people. All she can tell is that people are coming this way! It will be a while before they're close and they might just walk straight past. Martha looks at her swimsuit, and panics.

She grabs her bag, stuffs her clothes into the bag, not for one moment thinking that she could actually just get dressed and her entire problem would be solved. The towel is tied round her and she stumbles into her sandals. Bending over her bag, she hesitates. "What shall I do? Do I run back to the hotel? I'm still in my swimsuit though! What about..." Her desperate eyes take in the barracks with their big windows and black gaping doorways. "At least I could get changed and then go to the hotel... *later*." She was going to say, "...after those people have gone." Martha has just realised that if she had just sat down and dressed quickly, she would have been fine, and those young people (or whatever they are) would never have seen her. "Never mind, it's too late for that now," she mumbles. So, after another quick look to see if the group is still moving towards her, she scrambles off the sand, steps across the road, rushes up to the barracks, bypassing the first two, and goes straight to the one with a large window overlooking her beach.

Martha can feel resentment growing already. The group is definitely a bunch of youngsters, and for some reason she takes it very personally that they have driven her off *her* beach. Part of her realises that she was the one to make the decision to dash, but even so... Martha feels that she didn't really have a choice. "Nice and courageous," she hisses to herself, feeling shame warming her cheeks more than the sun. "Running away like that is really showing courage, trusting God to keep you safe." On the other hand, she has been in danger before whilst wearing a swimsuit, and although she wasn't particularly brave that day, she hadn't been safe either...

Martha rushes past the barracks, hardly bothering to glance through each window, wondering if they will be fit to get changed in. "I wouldn't want to get changed if the thing is totally rat-infested," she shivers, "or whatever animal they have living in deserted buildings here on Crete." The voices along the main road can be heard, and Martha almost runs up to the third barrack, and after a very quick glance round to make sure she can't be seen, dashes through the open gap that used to be the door. She turns round immediately, her eyes unable to see into the dark hut, and just peers out from behind the broken bits of doorframe to see if she can spot the youngsters. Her beach is half hidden by the other barrack; she will have to use the window for that.

Just as Martha decides to walk over to the window, she hears a tiny noise behind her, a shuffle. She spins round, drops her bag, stands rooted for a second, gasps, then half turns to run, takes a breath to scream – and finally just stops in sheer terror.

The sturdy-looking man right in front of her just looks at her with a still face, the tiniest smile making his appearance calm rather than stern. Martha keeps staring at him, whilst trying the tiniest shuffle backwards, hoping he won't notice the movement.

He notices straight away, and just by moving his head a fraction, Martha knows she'd better not move again. Her blood is pumping in her ears, in her head, making her cheeks feel like welsh coal on fire, and the rushing noise in her ears blocks out all other sounds, even the voices of the youngsters.

He knows what I'm planning to do! Who... what can I do? I need... Martha hasn't got the faintest idea what she needs or what to do, or even what she *can* do. The man blocks out all her thoughts and somehow his strength has completely drained all hers. Martha can feel her legs starting to shake, her shoulders cramping together, and she knows that she should do something. *Be courageous,* she manages to think, but that's as far as she gets. She has no idea how she is to be courageous in this situation. This man looks at least ten times stronger than William – and William almost killed her. This man could kill her with one finger!

Martha senses black spots moving in, her breathing increasingly becoming a struggle. She wonders if the young people will hear her if she screams, and whether they will get to her before this man kills her. She hesitates, then feels that it's her only option. She forces a slightly larger gulp of air into her lungs and opens her frozen lips a little.

But before she can make a sound, the man's eyes narrow slightly and his cool voice just says, "Don't."

That's it. One word, and all the air leaves her lungs, just like that. Her legs are now making her sway, and the man reaches out a hand without rushing in any way. The hardest fingers ever clamp round her elbow, steadying her and making her feel like she's going to pass out at the same time.

"You're alright, I won't eat you," he says, his voice still cool, his upper lip just curling up a tiny bit, making Martha think that he sees that she's a weak woman.

Well, he won't be the first, she thinks, wondering if he'll still keep her upright if she passes out completely...

He takes hold of her other elbow as well, and then forces her to squat down. "Just sit down a moment, before you *fall* down," the cool voice says, never changing, the eyes steady – and making her sit down doesn't seem to require the slightest bit of effort. This doesn't make Martha feel better at all. Her whole body is shaking now, and when she sees his mouth move, she realises that she can't hear him. No sounds get past the rushing and clanging noises in her ears and head.

His eyes narrow a little before his face smooths out, and one hand takes hold of her neck and the back of her head and he steadily pushes her head down. Martha resists, her breath now coming in panicked gasps, mixed with pathetic sobs. The hand doesn't slow down, and once he has her head pushed onto her knees, he holds it there.

It only takes Martha a short time to realise that, actually, it's helping. The noise in her ears stops, her breathing becomes calmer, and she doesn't feel as faint anymore either. Still, he holds her down a little longer until Martha does feel better. The shakes have shrunk down to mere trembles, and when he slowly lets go of her head, she looks up at him. He is sat down on one knee, the way soldiers do.

Somehow Martha's first thought is, *do soldiers know about artefacts and archaeology?* Then she makes herself listen to the man.

"That's better." He states it as a fact, but makes it half sound like a question, so Martha nods once, worried that she will pass out again if she is too enthusiastic with her head movements! "I didn't mean to scare you," the man says, "but I had to make sure you didn't let those kids know I was here. I'm doing my job; I don't want someone to mess it up."

Martha nods twice at this, wondering if the last bit was really meant as a threat, or whether she just read too much into that.

"You work at the resort..." The man's steady eyes look at her, and again Martha gives one quick nod. He raises one eyebrow, and says, "You didn't want those kids to see you on the beach?"

Martha swallows, thinking how much she has failed. So much for overcoming her fears, for being courageous, for trusting God with the outcome. It's obvious that her own fearfulness has landed her into a whole new mess. *I should have quickly dressed, waited for the youngsters to walk past, and nothing would have happened. Instead I'm in an empty barrack with a dangerous man, in my swimsuit, and nobody knows where I am.*

The shakes promptly come out in sympathy with her tears, and the man sighs – not in an unkind way, but in a manner that shows this situation is beyond him.

Martha remembers how William used to hate her tears, even after doing his best to make her cry in the first place. So she wills the tears to stop and clamps her arms round her middle, hoping to subdue the shakes. "I..." Her voice squeaky, she is determined to show even the tiniest sliver of courage. "I hate being round people in my swimsuit."

128

His mouth twists sideways in a smile, and his brown eyes soften. "Now you're stuck in a dark building in your swimsuit with a stranger!" he says, then grows serious again. "You have nothing to fear from me. I'm just doing my job."

Somehow, Martha believes him, and suddenly she wonders what his job is.

He must have seen the question in her wet eyes, for he says, "There are ancient artefacts coming onto the black market, so I have been asked to see if I can find the thief or thieves."

Martha gasps, then finds herself explaining things about Dimitris and Anna. The man listens, and Martha realises that he is the stillest man ever. She always moves, at least her fingers do: pushing up her glasses, tugging at her hair, wringing her fingers together – there is always movement, as well as the looking around, looking over her shoulder especially. This man, however, never seems to move unless necessary, and somehow it unnerves her a little and makes her feel like a fidgety child!

"I saw the lights too," he says, when she tells him about the lights she has seen. "That is why I have settled in these old barracks. I can see the islands well from here. I saw you on the boat," he adds, with another of those crooked smiles, making Martha feel hot in her face again. Little crow feet appear next to his eyes as he says, "Hey, that should make you feel better. After all, I'm the good guy!"

Martha looks away and says, "That's what all guys say, even when they are trying to kill you." The barrack goes quiet, and after a while she looks back at the man. He just sits there, unmoving, serious, his eyes calm, and she notices that this time he hasn't curled his lip at her, so at least he's not laughing at her. "Sorry," Martha swallows, pushing the words out one by one, "I didn't mean that... Well, I *did* mean it, I suppose... but I shouldn't be so bitter about it, and I shouldn't have said it to you." She rushes the words out before the tremor in her lips will distort the words. "My name is Martha," she adds, feeling that she ought to make some reconciliatory move.

"Nice to meet you, Martha. My name is Ron. And I do apologise for the scare I gave you," he says, his lopsided grin making him less scary.

18

MARTHA FEELS THE TREMORS STILL GOING through her and doesn't trust herself to get up. Ron shifts his weight onto one foot, and Martha just knows that he is starting to get restless. "I'm sorry," she says, her mouth struggling to form something similar to a smile. "I know you didn't mean to scare me; it's just that I wasn't particularly expecting anyone in this barrack. I have never seen you, even though I check all around me a lot."

Ron nods; again, his upper lip curls a little, and Martha feels the tremors increase straight away. Ron notices too… His eyes soften just a tiny bit, and he simply says that he noticed.

Martha blushes, tucking her hair behind her left ear, her hand shaking. "I know what you think of me," she starts, her voice just quivering a little, but Ron puts a hand up.

"It's not about what I think, Martha," he says. "I'm sure you have a reason for it. We all live with fears and deal with it in our own ways." His eyes have gone very dark all of a sudden, and the stillness of his face makes Martha feel very cold all of a sudden. "Again, I apologise," he carries on. "I knew that you were nervous, so I should have let you know I was in here before you came in. I wasn't totally expecting you to come in, and I was hoping to stay undetected."

Martha nods. Yes, having to find some thief that might be somewhere in this area can't be easy. She explains that she never liked the barracks, always sensed something was off, and only went in because she didn't want to meet those youngsters.

"Why were you scared of them?" Ron asks, looking at her, his own calmness making Martha feel less shaky.

Martha looks down. "I don't actually know, apart from not wanting them to see me in my swimming costume. It's only once I started running that I realised I could have got dressed before they even saw me. I wasn't thinking of them attacking me, I was just... scared, and I ran!" She can see his eyes looking at her, coming up without answers, and he just looks at her, one eyebrow raised. She swallows, and groans inside. *Really, Lord? I can't even remember properly...* She looks at her bare feet in sandals; even her toes tremble!

After a while Martha looks up and says, barely audible, "I have burns on my leg. My ex-husband said I forgot about my coffee and wanted to run off to draw, got up too quickly and spilt my coffee all over my leg..." She stops, looks away and shrugs.

Ron stays very quiet, and when Martha finally looks up to find him looking at her with his head tilted to one side, brown eyes intense, he finally says, "I find your word choice interesting."

Martha blushes, takes a deep breath and quietly explains that she can't remember the incident. She remembers that just before they were sitting down to have coffee, he had been angry with her.

"Do you like coffee?" Ron asks, one side of his mouth smiling.

Martha emphatically shakes her head. "As far as I know, I have never liked coffee. Neither of my parents really drank it, so I never got into it. William insisted I did, though."

Ron frowns, looking as confused as Martha feels most of the time.

"That is one of the reasons that I can't imagine spilling coffee over myself. I always accepted it though; it's only the last few days that I have started to realise that maybe I believed a lot of lies…"

Ron nods slowly and asks her what makes her think her ex told lies.

"Well, I have thought about some of the things that happened, and how he always blamed me. Maybe I was at fault, and maybe I should have confronted him, but he always put things in such a way that confused me. Like when I burned my legs, he took me to the doctor's the next day, explaining that I had spilled coffee over my legs and hidden it from him. He said I wanted him to look bad and get people's sympathy. It was the way he told the doctors and others that made it sound so plausible, but now that I'm away from him, I keep telling myself that I would never have drunk coffee. I like drawing, I really do, but I'm sure I have never been obsessed with it. I would certainly not forget guests, or even him, just to finish a drawing. As I work with coloured pencils, I can easily finish it another time. I don't have to mix paint and have different shades if it dries at different times!"

Ron nods again and says it's called *gaslighting*.

Martha looks up with a start. "Yes! That's the word my counsellor used!"

As soon as she mentions her counsellor, Ron's lip curls up. "One of my mates used one of *them,*" he says, and his voice makes it clear what he thinks of "them"...

Martha shrugs, and says that the woman was alright but wasn't that much help because Martha wasn't ready to believe her at that time. She was still too much under William's influence, so the counsellor's words just rolled off her. Now that she feels a little better, she has been going through her notes and sees a lot more stuff in them.

Ron stares out of the door opening and says, "You need a counsellor who knows what they're talking about. Some things can only be experienced, and sometimes you just have to find your own way out."

Martha looks at the dirty floor, thinking about that, weighing his words. *It's not easy to find your way out of complete darkness though,* she realises. "I think it's being here, having time to put things straight in my head, and time to think about what people have said, that has been helpful. I suppose counselling starts things off; it shows you how to analyse things and put your mind in order." Her mind runs through the last few days, and she adds, "I have a journal, which helps. Just listing good things from that day. Also, being the holiday rep has confronted me with some issues, so the first days I was sick a lot..." She cringes a bit. *This will go down well with Mr Strong!*

Ron snorts a little, but it's his lopsided grin that's in place, not the curled lip.

"Of course, a few times I just couldn't possibly be sick or pass out, so I had to fight through, and it has helped, I hope. That's then given me enough willpower and grace to think about stuff and my part in it all. I have started drawing again, something I had completely given up. William sharpened all the pencils from my favourite set and claimed that I had done it, but I know that I couldn't have done that, I just know. I will need to look into gaslighting. I recognise the word, but I couldn't accept what the counsellor said. The fact that he had taken me for a ride for more than a year made me feel such an idiot, I couldn't face it! The idea that I might have married an evil man would have shattered my dream. It was easier to accept William's version and see myself as the one to blame."

Ron looks thoughtful, and slowly says, "Yes, I can see that. That's quite often the case, I suppose." He looks quiet, withdrawn, for a bit, and Martha doesn't want to disturb him for he looks... sad. "Not all cases are clear cut, I suppose," he says after a bit, "and it's a good point to think about. It's easy to feel guilty for the wrong thing. Some people feel guilty quicker than others as well."

Martha nods. Yes, William obviously never did, but she did all the time; that's probably why their marriage lasted two years!

He looks at her again, genuine interest on his face. "What made you leave him though?"

Martha feels herself going cold all over, just like she always does when talking about that fateful afternoon. Taking a deep breath, she explains, "William became very angry. I can't even remember what about. I think he wanted to go for a special meal for our anniversary and I didn't look too happy because he was already drunk by then. I didn't think driving in his condition would be a bright idea. He really lost it, and pushed me so I fell over, hitting my jaw – and then he grabbed my throat." Martha stops, her whole body cold and shaking, wondering if she is going to be sick, and Ron leans forward, just putting one rough hand on her arm, just under her shoulder. That grounds her again and she manages to continue. "Just then my sister arrived at the house, because it was our wedding anniversary, and as she was nearby, she decided to pop in with some flowers... Just in time too, apparently. She took me to hospital, where an X-ray showed my cracked jaw and bruising on my neck. After that, my sister took me to their home to recover. I was so confused; it's been ages, and it's only now that I'm starting to see light at the end of the tunnel."

Ron nods. "That must have been tough. At least you're away from him now, setting up a life again, becoming your own person."

Martha nods, tries to smile, and wonders why she doesn't really feel free from William, wondering if Ron makes it sound too easy. On the other hand, lots of people have to go through things much worse, she supposes.

"It's finding a way forward," Ron continues, "and then just sticking to your choices and decisions. Having a job or goal is paramount, and then you just work towards that. There is always fear, of course; the important thing is to not be ruled by fear."

Again, Martha agrees, whilst a tiny part of her protests that there is no "just" about it. *If it were a case of just doing this or that, there wouldn't be a single person in need of counselling.* She sighs. *Of course, lots of people are probably like me, letting fear rule and seeing themselves as victims too often. No wonder Ron curled his lip at my story... It's not a story in which I especially glow with courage!* She looks at his very strong-looking arms, his solid body, the way he stands, the embodiment of strength. *If I were that strong, I wouldn't have such an issue with fear either!*

19

MARTHA LOOKS ROUND THE REST OF THE BAR-
rack for the first time, noticing the sleeping bag neatly
rolled up in a corner and a large backpack next to it. It's
all very neat, and ready to go.

Ron sees her looking and smiles. "Ready to go at a
moment's notice," he explains. "As soon as I have a solid
lead, I might have to leave."

Martha shivers. She would hate that – not knowing
when you'll go, or where... Going to Crete for a month
was bad enough; she had studied the pictures and maps
endlessly, and even then, she had been almost ill with
panic before she got here! *No wonder the guy is fearless,
happy to take every day in his stride.*

Ron grins. "I can't offer you a drink, I'm afraid. I've
just got water and one cup."

Martha laughs, amazed that he manages to make her
feel so relaxed. If someone had told her that she would be
sitting in a dark barrack in her swimsuit with a dangerous-
looking man, she would probably have passed out on the
spot! She isn't sure whether that says more about Ron or
about her improved state of mind...

Ron gets out a tiny notebook and a pencil, looking a
lot more serious now.

Martha shivers a tiny bit, as his intense face somehow makes him look a formidable opponent. She just hopes that she stays on his good side...

"What time did you see the lights?" He looks at her, pencil hovering.

Martha thinks about it and gives the time, explaining how the lights seemed to move over a little and then disappear.

Ron nods, looks down on his notes, then his head comes up quickly and he says, "You're sure?" His eyes glint, and Martha feels her own heartbeat speeding up.

"Definitely, and the second time I double-checked the time, because I sent Anna a text to tell her about it."

Ron looks pleased, and scribbles away in his tiny notebook again.

Martha cringes a little. *Who holds a pencil like that?* "Does that mean the thief hides on Dia?" she asks, feeling like a detective, her mind wondering, forcing the sweet guy with a goatie out of her mind.

Ron shrugs and explains that Dia is bigger, and therefore will have better hiding places, but the theft seems to come from the smaller islands.

Martha thinks about the underwater amphorae. "It's easy to get to them," she says, "and Anna says there are so many of them, it's impossible to see whether some have been stolen. Although, I'm sure if people took pictures, you could compare them every few days?"

Ron smiles a little and explains that it would take too long, as there are underwater artefacts everywhere, so the effort of taking pictures then comparing them every few days isn't worth it. No, he just needs to get his eyes on the guy – and find out if there even is a guy.

"I suppose it could just be tourists, wild camping or something," Martha agrees. "Especially if the lights are always on Dia and the theft isn't." She thinks of the underwater amphora she drew, and suddenly asks, "How do they know the artefacts were from around here? Don't they all look the same?"

Ron laughs. "Yes, *I* think they do. But I'm not an expert, and apparently, the experts can tell where the stuff comes from. It was quite a job to find out it was an amphora that had been underwater, as they clean up nicely, but after a long time they managed to get a list of facts together, which is where they got me involved. It's somewhere round here, so that's why I'm holed up in this place." Martha shivers again, and Ron laughs. "It's definitely not the worst hiding place I have had." His face is smiling but his eyes look a bit sad all of a sudden.

Martha tries to sound a bit upbeat as she tells Ron that her favourite hiding place as a child was the little cupboard that collected post and had the electric meter. Of course, she wouldn't ever hide in such a tight, dark space like that now, not for a million pounds!

Ron smiles his funny lopsided smile, and Martha is pleased to see his eyes smiling as well. For all his strength and fearlessness, there are things that make him sad, too, and to her shame it comforts her! The fact that this man is not above hurt and grief shouldn't make her feel relieved, but it does.

"Wouldn't it be better to hide on Paximadi then?" she asks, thinking about the tiny rocky dot in the blue sea.

Ron agrees, but explains that it's too hard to hide long-term, what with the tourists coming and going.

Martha understands. "Although, it's a bit quieter now, as it's later in the season. I suppose this place is easier, as you get a better overview." She shivers again, this time simply because she is starting to feel cold. She checks her watch, and looks up, feeling rushed and confused as well as awkward. "I need to go," she blurts out. "Dinner will be waiting for me." Suddenly she feels scared all over again. *Will Ron let me go, just like that? Or will he refuse to let me go until he has finished his job? After all, I might give his hiding place away...*

Ron just nods, picking up her bag for her and handing it to her.

Martha feels her face heating up when she catches his eyes. *He knows exactly what I was thinking,* she moans to herself. She looks at him. "I won't let anyone know you're here, you know that? Also, I could bring you a hot coffee the next time I'm on the beach... I have coffee and tea facilities in my apartment." She smiles to herself when she sees his face light up! They shake hands, and soon she finds herself walking back to the resort, constantly looking round, as she really doesn't want to meet or see anybody like this.

Martha holds onto her towel with one hand, feeling exposed, but in too much of a rush to stop at the beach to get dressed. Ron can see her there anyway, and she would feel silly slipping into her dress.

As soon as she gets to her own room, the shaking suddenly increases and she has to lower herself onto the floor in a quick effort to stop herself from collapsing. "I was in the dark with a man, all by myself," she squeaks, her whole body convulsing. Martha lunges towards the bathroom on hands and knees, and just makes it in time.

Wiping her mouth afterwards, she feels so weak – almost too weak to shake. She just lies on the cool tiles, her body trembling from fear and weakness. "In my swimsuit," she groans, then remembers that at least she had her towel round her waist. "What will I do next time?" She suddenly remembers that her private beach is no longer private! "He has seen me every time, seen me getting into the water and everything... Now I can never go back in the sea..." Self-pity makes her eyes fill up with tears, and she can feel resentment growing at the same time. "That was my only option for a swim, and now that's gone."

She gasps suddenly. "Actually, no, I don't really have to stop. I mean, maybe I should use this as a chance to overcome my fear. After all, he has seen me already; he was there all the time. I didn't know it, but he was, so in theory nothing has changed. It's me that has changed, but maybe this is just another opportunity to grow. Yes, I should really accept it that way. Lord, I don't know if I can though, I'm not strong enough, so I will need to lean on You. Can I do that, without..."

She stops. *Without what? Without God disappointing me? Letting me down? Is that how I see His care of me during my marriage? That I trusted Him, but He let me down? Or was it that I didn't actually trust Him, lean on Him, but lived my own way during my marriage?* She sighs, another rabbit warren to sort through... "It's never ending!" She rolls her eyes, feeling a spark of bitterness. "Who else has to do so much sorting out? Why did it happen to me, and what if I just want to be a normal person, living my life, having a job..."

Martha stares ahead, feeling her anger towards William more clearly than ever. She realises that she feels her resentment towards him grow each time she realises what a long road she still has ahead of herself. "I was never like this," she says, an edge to her voice. "I loved my family, my friends, my drawing and life itself. I would never have guessed that I would turn out like this, some feeble woman, sitting on her bathroom floor, throwing up every time she talks to a man." Tears come afresh, and Martha says bitterly, "I hate you William, for what you have done to me." Then she stops, and adds, "I hate myself, for allowing you to do this to me," which she feels is probably more to the point. Her mind drifts off along that line, but she doesn't dare to blame God for not protecting her because she didn't really lean on Him, trust Him or even ask Him! "I should have done, Lord, but then... I felt You were on his side. After all, he was so active in church, and people kept telling me how godly my husband was... I even believed him when he told me that I had to obey him; after all, he was the head of the house... I should have thought about it more, and... and prayed more."

Martha pulls a face. Yes, she got it so wrong and it was really her own fault. On the other hand, she is now free from William, this is a new day, and she has learned more. "So, tomorrow" – her voice sounds stronger, more upbeat – "tomorrow I will go to my beach, and swim and draw and whatnot. I will also bring hot coffee for Ron. I just need to be very careful when bringing it to him..." She suddenly smiles. Yes, she's going to be brave, and it feels a bit like an adventure, and she's determined to make herself enjoy it! On legs that feel only a little bit rubbery, she walks to her Lifeline and fills in the last few events and Ron's name, as well as her plans for tomorrow. "I didn't ask how he likes his coffee," she realises, then decides to just take it black. "Strong guys probably drink strong coffee," she giggles, amazing herself with her sense of excitement!

20

MARTHA WAKES UP WONDERING WHAT THE situation was today in which she was going to confront some fear and overcome it. All through breakfast she tries to remember and can feel her anxiety ever increasing. "There has to be something; I just can't remember!" In the end she decides to look in her Lifeline to find out. When she sees it's "going to the beach, bring coffee to R and carry on as normal", she gasps. "I'm not sure I can…" Martha tries to take some deep breaths, but the idea of getting into the water knowing that Ron is watching her makes her shoulders tense up. "On the other hand, he's done it for a while now, and…" The difference is that she didn't know he was looking. "I'm sure he wasn't staring," she tries to tell herself. She remembers his stillness, and his eyes that see too much…

Martha takes her time over her breakfast and her morning clients. In the end there is no reason to stay away any longer, and she slowly makes a thermos with black coffee. She hesitates, looking round her apartment, as if some very important appointment will spring up! Finally, there is nothing keeping her anymore, and Martha starts off down the dusty road. By the time she gets to her beach, she is out of breath, her legs feeling wobbly and her shoulders tight. She puts her stuff on the beach, hesitates, looks round and round, but avoids looking at the barracks. There isn't another person in sight, and still she hesitates. In the end she can't avoid looking at the old barracks any longer. Just as she lets her eyes wander over to the old buildings with their dark, gaping windows, she spots Ron. He comes from behind the nearest building, and quickly crosses the road. Martha has to swallow, as his quick, confident stride doesn't improve her own confidence at all!

"Morning, Martha," he smiles at her, his mouth lopsided as always, and Martha just has to smile back, hoping he doesn't notice her shaking hands. From the way he narrows his eyes ever so slightly, she guesses that her hopes have just been dashed... She quickly grabs the flask and hands it to him.

"Thank you. You remembered!"

His smile is genuine, and his eyes sparkle, making her stomach flip, then churn. Martha says shyly that she wrote it down in her Lifeline.

"Your Lifeline?" he asks, looking confused, and she explains that she has started a special notebook for absolutely everything, as she found that her memory wasn't working at all. It caused so many embarrassing moments and forgotten details that in the end she decided to carry a notebook with her at all times. "My ex-husband always reminded me of everything, and later my counsellor said that because of the gaslighting, my memory wasn't working properly. My ex-husband said, for example, that we had arranged for certain visitors, without me knowing. So when they turned up, he would say that I didn't care about anything or anyone, only my drawing. I believed him..."

Ron nods, and says that the whole idea of gaslighting is to make the other person believe it…

Martha shrugs. "I can't believe I was that stupid… It's taken me ages to understand, and still I find it all really hard." She wriggles her toes into the sand, feeling suddenly awkward. She wonders what Ron will think. *Here he is, listening to me rabbiting on and on about my issues, and all he wanted was his coffee!*

Ron watches her, whilst simultaneously scanning the sea, and explains that it all takes time. "You'll get there," he says, his voice sounding confident, making Martha wish it were true. "It might take time, but most good things take time. It's training your mind again."

Martha nods. *Yes, so many things have to be revised in my head.*

"That's the hardest part, and once you're clear that ideas need revising, you have made a good start," he smiles, and Martha is relieved that he hasn't curled his upper lip, although she can somehow sense the little ripple of impatience underneath his words and his smile. "There is your friend's boat," he says, pointing with a nod across to the island.

Martha manages to see the tiny speck that must be a boat. She wonders how he knows it's Dimitris' boat, then rolls her eyes at herself. "He's just saying that to show he's in charge and knows his job." Just like William tried a few times to explain to her about superior pencils… She looks up to find Ron looking at her with a very small grin, and without saying anything, he pulls a tiny set of binoculars from his pockets and hands it to her.

Martha feels the heat in her face, annoyed and embarrassed with his ability to somehow read her mind!

She trains the binoculars on the little dot, giving a gasp when the very powerful tool shows up Dimitris' boat clearly...

Ron laughs a little when she hands back the binoculars, and he says, "No need to trust me blindly, you know. Hopefully, I'm nothing like your ex, but only you will know."

Martha shrugs, feeling uncomfortable. *Why wouldn't he be like William? The way confidence pours off him, the way he clearly detests weakness...* She has to admit that he seems to have a lot of self-control, which would probably stop him from making the same mistakes as William, but even so...

After a while Ron goes back to his barrack, having scanned the area carefully, and Martha stops herself from watching him disappear. She turns to the water, hesitating, wondering whether she should just sit on her towel and draw... The water looks inviting though, and it's hot, and her face is hotter than ever when the blue of the water reminds her of sapphires. Sapphire Beach and sapphire rings... An image of Ron's brown eyes floats through her head, and her stomach twists and turns in protest. She shivers, then quickly takes her clothes off and walks to the water in her swimsuit, forcing her mind to stay focussed on the warm water, the little fish, the hot sand and the bright sun... Not once does she allow her mind to wander off towards old ramshackle barracks or men with lopsided grins!

When Martha comes back to her towel after a while, she makes a careful note in her Lifeline, as she feels pleased that she managed to get into the water, knowing that Ron might well be watching her! "That's one up for me," she says. "I'm not a victim…" Soon she is dry, and busy drawing.

She doesn't hear Ron's footsteps coming across the road. He stops a little bit behind her, tempted to surprise her. Then he remembers her fear when they met the first time, how she was shaking and almost passed out, so he stops and gives a little cough. Martha's reaction stuns him. She spins round, gasping for breath, dropping her paper and pencil. She half scrambles away, shaking all over, her eyes wild with terror. Ron stands very still, and keeping his voice low, just calls her name, without moving. Martha stops scrambling, and the sheer terror in her eyes dies down a little, her breath still coming in erratic gasps and her body shaking too hard for her to get up.

Ron lowers himself down, just a little closer to her. "Martha, it's alright; it's just me. I came to return your flask." He makes sure to look her in the eyes, forcing himself not to look at her legs.

Martha nods, or at least tries to, tears blurring her vision. Somehow, Ron's brown eyes manage to get through, which doesn't help…

"Is there something I can do to help?" His voice is calm, and Martha feels a tiny flicker of relief that he isn't curling his lip at her…

She shakes her head, and nods when Ron spots her water bottle and offers it to her. He doesn't get much closer to her, just reaches the bottle over to her. Martha struggles to get the bottle, as her hands are shaking too much to get a good grip on it. Ron is patient though, and just holds on to her water until she manages to get it. Somehow, she gets the bottle top off and takes a few sips, embarrassment burning through her. All the while Ron stays still and silent, not rushing her, not trying to make her feel better, no suggestions of what she ought to do, and Martha feels beyond grateful.

"Thank you," she says very quietly after a while. "Thank you for not trying to fix me. I'm sorry, I just hadn't heard you coming." She blushes a bit, for her reaction was over-the-top for someone being surprised...

Ron passes her the flask, his grin genuine. "I loved the coffee; it saved my day," he says. "I miss my coffee when I don't get any!" He looks at her, his smile turning a bit warmer, and he says, "You did well today. I wasn't sure if you would swim knowing I was nearby..."

Martha pulls a face and admits that she wasn't sure either.

"There you are, see, another decision in the right direction," he grins and shakes his head when Martha says that her panic attack rather undid the courage bit. "No, a step doesn't get undone just because your next step wasn't as brave or clear." His voice is confident, his brown eyes never leaving hers.

Martha shrugs, but deep inside she accepts his words, thinking about them, feeling comforted by them. She manages a feeble smile herself, and thanks him, admitting that she still has such a long way to go, she doesn't know if she'll ever get there!

"You will, but one step at the time. You can't force healing." His smile has gone and his eyes are dreamy, as if his mind has wandered off to other sandy stretches.

That evening Martha writes in her journal, listing the blessings, and in her gaudy notebook she writes down what has happened these last two days. She looks out across the water, and when she spots the sudden light on Dia, a wild plan comes up. "Why not? I will be careful, and I'm tired of being afraid all the time. I hate the pitiful looks at home and the way Ron curls his lip at me. I know I have been weak, and I know I still have a way to go. I'm an overcomer though, not a victim. I will do it, and that will make people look at me in a different way. It will be a good way to prove I'm a victor. I know I can do this; after all, if I do things right there will be no danger. It will show initiative and courage and it will help me in the future as well. It's like Ron said; I need to have a goal. This is a goal, a purpose, a step forward."

21

MARTHA HAS A RESTLESS NIGHT, HER PLAN keeping her awake. Whenever she falls asleep things go badly wrong in her dream. Images of burning coffee, swimsuits, brown eyes and hands throttling her follow her round glistening blue inlets, filled with terra cotta amphorae. She is tired at breakfast but determined to put her plan into action, and as soon as she has finished with her clients, she takes the bus to Iraklion. In the bus she looks back on the last trips and realises that getting the bus to Iraklion is becoming normal; nothing shakes or trembles! She feels pleased and smiles a little when getting off the bus.

Martha spots the bench where she had her panic attack the first time and suddenly finds herself curling her lip! *Oh no, I'm copying him,* she gasps, shocked by her own response! Then she realises that she referred to Ron as "him" as if he were a large part of her life... Martha feels her shoulders tense up and suddenly doesn't feel like sneering at herself anymore. The panic is obviously not that far away from her after all... Only by reminding herself that she came on the bus and into the city without problems can Martha calm herself down. She walks quickly to Anna's shop, hoping the young woman will be there.

She is, and Anna smiles warmly when Martha walks in. "Hi Martha, how are you? Dimitris is so happy with your beautiful drawing! His friends are all jealous, and some customers have been asking for copies!"

Martha laughs, feeling an unfamiliar thrill – one that she used to have a long time ago; the thrill of her work being recognised and appreciated. She remembers William's face and reaction when he saw her work displayed and the price tag underneath... Her smile wobbles a little, then shines even brighter. *He tried; he really tried, but I'm back up!* She explains to Anna that Dimitris is welcome to make copies to sell.

"Oh, thank you!" Anna beams. "He will be so happy! Are you sure?"

Martha nods, feeling grateful for Anna's care and the way she double-checks.

"It is such a good drawing," Anna says, her kind face looking at Martha with admiration, "but I can understand as an artist that you don't want your work just copied like that."

Martha smiles, and repeats that she really doesn't mind. "In fact," she adds, "I need to ask Dimitris for a favour. I have a plan, but I need him to give me a lift." Martha explains her plan and Anna's smile has gone completely by the time she has finished. "Look, I will be very careful. Nobody will know of my plan; only you," she says. "Nobody is to know about Ron because he's on a secret mission. I really don't want to mess up his job, but I know I can help, and it would be great if I can find out more." Anna looks grave, and Martha quickly adds, "I know it could be dangerous, but I'm just going to make sure I'm hidden somewhere, and I'll just watch, that's all.

I want to show to myself that I can do this, and I want to help." She manages to swallow in "Ron" just in time. Martha can feel her cheeks warming up a little, and by the look in Anna's eyes, her friend realises that there is a name missing...

"So... this Ron..." Anna begins, her eyes looking mischievous. "I will have to meet him one day."

Martha grins and suddenly giggles. Then she shivers and struggles against tears. Anna's face looks serious again, and once Martha has blown her nose, Martha admits that Ron scares her more than anything. "He is so confident and stands really tall. He looks very strong and hardly ever moves – you know? – really still. He sees everything," she says, her voice still shaking a bit. "He seems alright, but he scares me. His hands look really powerful, and I know that when he hits me or pushes me or grabs me, I won't have a chance."

Anna looks stunned at this and asks Martha why she thinks Ron will hurt her.

"I don't know... Maybe if I annoy him or something goes wrong; I don't know. He dislikes tears and I know he finds me annoying when I panic," she says, remembering his curled lip.

Anna looks at Martha – *really* looks – and her eyes suddenly fill with tears. "Oh Martha, I'm sorry," she whispers. "I don't know your whole story, but it's obviously left scars! He sounds safe; he's probably Special Forces or something. And Martha, not once has a man hit me or hurt me," she adds softly.

Martha shrugs a little and admits that before her marriage it wouldn't have even occurred to her either... She has to agree that Ron doesn't sound like a dangerous man; it's just that he looks so capable, and his iron fingers remind Martha of hands round her throat…

Anna's face brightens a little, and she asks, "So what does he look like? Is he tall and good looking?"

Martha feels a giggle bubbling up and describes Ron, admitting that it's the sapphire ring comment that makes her break out in a cold sweat every time.

Anna laughs then. "I don't actually know anyone that got married based on their time at Sapphire Beach, although there could be visitors from the resort that met and married later. Anyway, I love sapphires," she adds.

Martha agrees that she does too, and has never liked ruby, but her ex had insisted on a huge ruby ring – and since then she has *really* detested rubies… They laugh, and Martha says that it's not just to help Ron; she just feels she ought to overcome her fears, face them head on.

Anna nods slowly, then says, "Now, about your plan… I don't know – it sounds dangerous… but if you're sure… I just can't imagine staying on the island after dark. You realise it will be quite hard to hide? There are no trees on Paximadi. What will you do if something happens? Are you absolutely sure about this?" Yes, Martha is definitely sure, and in the end, Anna agrees to set it up with Dimitris. "Once he knows, he won't do it though, I'm sure. We'll have to let him think it's a prank or something, and hopefully he won't ask too many questions… I can't lie, obviously!"

Martha agrees, and Anna promises to text her, and hopefully will pick Martha up the next morning.

Martha gets out her Lifeline, to start on a list with things to take. "It will be cold at night, and I will need a torch, and stuff to eat…"

Anna nods, and says that the best place would be a space between rocks, or a small cave.

"Yes," Martha agrees, "it will have to be somewhere where I can see the amphorae though. Now, I'm fairly confident it's not done on the side facing the mainland. If that were the case, Ron would have spotted them, I'm sure!"

Anna agrees that it's bound to be the part towards the side where their boat was moored for a while.

Martha nods. "Yes, I just hope I can spot their light."

Anna explains that Dimitris has a pair of night vision goggles that she can borrow.

"Great idea," Martha says, feeling the excitement growing, as well as her fear. She is not keen on the dark, and to be alone with a criminal on a tiny island makes her shoulders tense up and her hands grow cold and clammy. She is determined though, and she tries to tell herself that God will bless her efforts to overcome her fears and that she will go trusting in His strength to keep her safe...

The list complete, Martha leaves the shop, gets some food from around Iraklion's shops, another bottle of water for in the bus, and then slowly makes her way back to the bus station. Just as she gets in the bus, there is a text from Anna, telling her it's all arranged and Anna will pick her up in the morning... Martha is thrilled, then struggles the rest of the journey back with fear.

In her apartment she packs her bag, her hands shaking; and when she packs a small but sharp kitchen knife, she has to run to the bathroom to throw up. "What am I thinking," she whispers, her forehead on the cool tiles. "I'm taking a knife in case I get face to face with a dangerous criminal who's probably got a gun or something like that!" She picks up her phone, planning to text Anna to cancel the wild scheme, but stops. "No, I will do this, and hopefully, I will overcome my fears. I will take the knife, just in case I struggle with one of the food wrappers," she says, trying to make herself believe this to be the case.

Martha puts her phone on the charger, determined to keep the battery fully charged as long as possible. Then, looking at her packed bag, she puts her hands on her hips and makes herself say proudly, "Here we are; I'm not a victim, I'm a victor. I'm strong, I can do all things, and I will show..." She almost said "Ron" again. "I will show *everyone* that I'm not a victim, but a victor. Once I show them where and how it's done, the big guys can just go and nab the thief."

Martha avoids thinking about relying not on her own strength, but on God's strength. She avoids thinking about all the things that could go wrong. She is determined to be brave and won't allow her mind to think about whether this is the best way to go about it.

In her journal she finds it hard to find blessings for the day; her mind is spinning too much. In her gaudy notebook she writes down her day's events and also her plans... She has thought about it quite carefully, she feels, but writing it down doesn't lessen her anxiety at all. On the contrary, her plan written down looks rather dangerous and foolhardy. "I know what I'm doing. I'll just stay hidden, out of sight, and Dimitris will pick me up the following day," she says, making herself feel excited. "It's just shakes because I'm so excited about this adventure," she insists, knowing full well that after her marriage the word 'adventure' had absolutely no appeal;

living a very calm, structured and predictable life was her main goal for the next few decades... So far, coming to Crete is the largest jump she has made, and even that was done carefully, with lots of preparation. Whilst here she has managed to form a routine, enjoying the quiet, structured days. Now she is throwing that out and going completely against her life's goal.

Martha gets up abruptly, knowing that if she thinks about it anymore, she will pull out.

22

THE FOLLOWING MORNING MARTHA STRUGgles with breakfast. Just a bit of toast and black tea will have to do, because just looking at other food makes her stomach do backflips. Anna comes to pick her up, her face serious.

"You are sure, aren't you?" she asks, her eyes dark and worried.

Martha nods and makes her mouth smile. She explains that she will just hide, not move, and just watch what happens.

"I hope nothing happens, to be honest. These thieves are evil because there is money involved. Do you think Ron will guess what you're going to do?"

Martha shakes her head, and has to giggle, in spite of the stress. Her face heats up remembering the panic attack he set in motion. *No, Ron would never expect me to do something as... brave as this.* She insists on calling it "brave" in her mind because alternative words present themselves much more readily.

Anna laughs when Martha explains why she doesn't think Ron will have any idea what she is planning to do. "I hope he'll appreciate it. You know what guys can be like..." she says, and Martha nods – yes, she really knows what men are like. She shivers and is determined not to mess up or make mistakes.

Dimitris is glad to see her, and thanks her again for the beautiful drawing. "Thank you for allowing me to make copies and sell them," he says, explaining that he will do so as soon as possible. "Anna knows someone who will make great quality copies," he adds, busy sorting out the boat ready to go.

There are two young couples on the vessel, who hardly look up when Anna and Martha climb aboard. Martha is glad, as she needs to be able to get off the boat unseen. She settles in near the back, squeezed into a corner. Dimitris starts the engine and soon the boat glides across the blue sea.

Martha looks at the water, her stomach juices joining in with the waves, sloshing and gurgling. She knows she will be sick soon unless she distracts herself enough. So she wanders over to Dimitris and asks if there is another drawing he would like. His face lights up immediately. "Yes please, Martha! Maybe one from the boat's interior?"

Martha nods. *Yes, the boat is quite quaint, and the coiled rope, diving goggles, picnic basket and wooden seats make for a lovely picture.* She gets her paper and pencils out and soon she can feel her body calming down. Her heartbeat is still faster than usual, and she struggles to keep her mind in check, but her fingers hardly tremble at all, the feel of the smooth pencil in her hand relaxing and familiar. The sound of the pencil scratching the paper is a very soothing noise, and she actually finds herself struggling to stay awake!

By lunchtime most of the drawing is done, and Martha is relieved, for now that the time to sneak off the boat is nearer, her body is starting to react. She just nibbles on some food, feeling a little annoyed with her own weakness as the picnic consists of gorgeous food again!

Anna and Martha try to stay away a little from the young couples because Martha doesn't want any questions asked at the end of the day. Anna looks worried but tries to sound as upbeat as possible, determined to make Dimitris believe it's just a dare.

Dimitris was not impressed by the idea, but the women assured him that Martha would be very careful, and that it would just be for one night. Even now, though, he looks at Martha with concern all over his face.

"I promise to be careful and stay hidden," Martha says again. "It's just a dare a colleague made me – whether I could survive a night on a deserted island near the coast. She has to treat me to a meal of my choice if I manage it! Anyway, it's a full moon – or almost full at least – and I'd love to draw that as well."

Dimitris nods, but looks unsure. Martha is glad that he doesn't ask how she plans to draw in the night, as she knows she'll be too scared to use her torch. Also, there is the tiny chance of the thieves being nearby, and torchlight would give her away. Earlier Dimitris mentioned the thief, or thieves, but Martha pointed out that the lights were on Dia island and she wanted to hide on Paximadi. "I'll hide near the cove where we stopped and the ladies had their swim," she says. "That way it will be easier for you to pick me up. There are so many rocks and small caves, I'm sure I can find somewhere comfortable to shelter for the night."

When Dimitris moors the boat in the little sheltered area, the two couples are soon in the water, swimming and diving. They are thrilled to see the many amphorae, and Dimitris keeps an anxious lookout to make sure they don't touch them. Their voices sound happy and carefree, and Martha somehow feels a little stab of envy. They seem so free, smiling and happy, just enjoying the holiday. She grabs her bag, puts the pencils and paper away, and adds the night vision goggles, carefully storing them in the bag. She looks over the edge of the boat towards the couples. The last thing she wants is to be seen in her swimsuit. She also wants to make sure they don't see her getting off the boat and onto the island.

Anna comes over to her. "Are you all fixed?" Her face is very serious, and Martha nods, grinning her bright smile.

Martha's glasses are as high up her nose as they will go, and she has evidently been tucking her hair behind her ear a lot during the ride as it is already darker from becoming greasy. Her shoulders ache from the tension she has been fighting. Soon she is just wearing her swimsuit, with her clothes and sandals in her bag. Anna holds on to it whilst she climbs down the little boat ladder into the water. The water is warm, coming almost up to her neck, and the gentle movement of the waves feels calming.

"It's like getting into the bath," Martha smiles, her lips less frozen than they were. "Thanks, Anna!"

Anna carefully hands her large bag to her, checking once again with a whisper that Martha is absolutely sure, and reassuring her that she can easily pull out and come back aboard the boat...

Martha shakes her head. "No, but thank you! I will see you in the morning, alright?" Dimitris only has an afternoon trip booked, so he and Anna will be picking her up early in the morning. She hopes she'll be back at the hotel in time for breakfast. The idea of more food doesn't make her feel better at all, but she knows that she will be ravenous once the whole ordeal is over.

It's hard work swimming quietly to the shore. Even though Martha's bag is fully waterproof, it is still awkward and heavy to carry. Her arms are soon aching, but she somehow makes it.

She has to sit for a while to catch her breath and she can feel the shakes taking over, her stomach accusing her as well, but she forces herself to think of it as an adventure, something to help... *Well, to help, that's it.* She remembers Ron's advice: she just needs to conquer her fears, set a goal and go for it. "So, my goal is to spend a night hiding nearby, watch the little bay, and not be sick." She giggles a little, imagining Ron with his confidence and strength making a similar list for staying in the dark barrack. *"Watch the enemy, keep an eye out for the woman on my beach, and do not throw up in a corner of the barrack every time a rat runs round in the night."* Martha pulls a face, suddenly not liking the idea that she is thinking about the man, imitating his calm voice and everything. She shivers, and in order to force the image of his brown eyes and lopsided grin from her mind, she decides that it's time to move on and find somewhere to spend the night.

Hidden from sight behind a jutting-out rock, she quickly dries herself a bit and then walks carefully away from the little beach. There isn't really a path, but Martha manages to climb over some rocks, and after searching around a bit, finds two rocks making a little shelter. Between them, a windblown shrub is clinging on for dear life, and Martha leans against the rather prickly stem. "This will do," she mutters, needing to hear her voice. "Rocks on either side, small brush behind me, view across the little bay... I should be well hidden, and I can see quite a lot." The rocks certainly seem to form a perfect hiding place, keeping her out of sight. She stores her bag, and just pulls out the little towel again and slips out from between the rocks.

On a smooth rock next to the hiding place, Martha lies down in the sun, basking and letting the hot sun dry her at the same time. She dozes off a little in the heat but wakes up with a start when she hears Dimitris' voice down below calling the couples. She can't hear the exact words, but she guesses that is what he is doing because she can hear their answering voices. Soon after, she can hear the boat's engine start up.

By now Martha is dry as cork, so staying low, she slips into her dress and crawls into the little space between the rocks. She watches the boat disappear, and her whole body reacts by shaking violently. "I'm a victor," she whispers, trying to keep her breathing smooth to stop the sickness from engulfing her. "I can't be sick here," she groans. "I'm not a victim. I can do this; it will be morning before I know it." Martha checks her phone, not surprised to see she has no signal. Surprisingly enough, the holiday rep phone has a tiny line of the signal flicker on and off, and Martha hopes that it will work should she need it...

23

MARTHA WATCHS THE BRIGHT-COLOURED boat for as long as she can, and the sudden loss she feels when it disappears really hits her. For a few moments she stays sitting still, unmoving, just trembling a little. The air is very quiet; not a sound can be heard – just a few cicadas further inland having a competition, it seems. Martha sits between the rocks, her back against the rough trunk of the small bush, not moving at all. After a while she realises that she is getting stiff, as well as more anxious, so with determined movements she pulls the paper and pencils from her bag. The boat interior looks great, so Martha spends some time finishing the drawing. Looking at the picture makes her feel very alone and vulnerable. She misses Anna and her kindness; she misses Dimitris and his warm smile. She's stuck here by herself on a deserted island, waiting for dangerous criminals, and only Anna and Dimitris know where she is.

Martha has to put the pencil down; her hands have started to shake too much. "What have I done?" she whispers. "What was I thinking? Even Ron stays well away from the island, and I have no training – nothing – and I have gone to the island by myself; nobody I can contact…" She thinks of her phone without any signal. "I can't do anything," she groans. "I can't even change my mind!" The panic is growing, her shoulders tense and pulled together; Martha feels cold and clammy, rocking herself in despair, frozen fingers clutched desperately round her locket. Somehow, she has chosen to spend the night on a tiny island off the Cretan coast, hoping to catch sight of criminals…

When the shakes have slowed down to trembles, Martha tidies away her paper and pencils. She feels too queasy to do any drawing. In order to settle her stomach, or at least try to, she nibbles on some crackers. The crunchy texture helps, and it does put some weight in her stomach. Martha is amazed to see the sun almost down now. *That went fast! Soon it will be dusk.* The trembles seem to grow in strength once more. She wonders whether the criminals will come when it's dark. *Will they come at all, or am I wasting time and bucketloads of energy for nothing?* Martha's thoughts just spin round and round, her shoulders all hunched up and tight.

The sunset is beautiful though, and in the face of those incredible colours, Martha half forgets the reason she is here. She grabs her phone and takes a few pictures of the sun glowing in the water, of the waves gurgling in the little cove, the sun giving them a beauty unheard of. She relaxes in spite of it all. *After all, Lord, I have come to do this in Your strength.* A tiny niggle in the back of her head quietly reminds her that Pastor Volodya probably didn't have dangerous missions in mind…

Martha is determined though, and sits back, a stubborn look on her face. Darkness moves in, and she can feel real fear moving into her heart as well. She hates the dark at the best of times, and there are none of her routines to see her through, no familiar actions to soothe and make her feel safe.

Martha looks at the dark sky, her thoughts drifting to her sister's house in the Cotswolds, myriads of stars flung across the sky. Martha felt so small, so insignificant, and God felt so far away, unapproachable. Bitterness and anger grew in her heart each day. Her jaw was sore, eating was painful, and she could never erase the images taken of her throat. Simon was a kind brother-in-law but as a policeman he made sure they had evidence. Louisa and Simon took pictures, stored her X-ray showing her cracked jaw, and listened to her crying and throwing up... Martha pulls a face. *No idea why they stayed so patient, and I didn't even understand their problem with William. It just made me feel worse, the way they talked about him, as if he were a criminal, whereas I had obviously incited him...* Even now, Martha struggles to accept that William was guilty of abuse, the word making her stomach shrivel. *I lived in fear and didn't realise I should have put my trust in God, not my own ability to please William. If I had stayed close to God, I would have seen what he was doing, I'm sure.* She knows there is still so much bitterness inside her, but she has started to let go. "He makes me a victim all over if I let him ruin each day," she whispers, then shivers in the cold air.

The island was very hot in the day and the stones still have some of the heat that they're passing on to her. The temperature is steadily dropping though. Martha quietly pulls her jumper from her bag as well as the blanket. Just when she has installed herself again, she hears noises. She goes completely quiet, holding her breath.

A little boat glides into the cove, hardly making any ripples at all. Martha moves very slowly and pulls the night vision goggles from her bag. She gives a tiny gasp when she looks through them; it's quite spooky! The colours are weird, and the men move like green aliens. Martha fiddles a little bit with the settings, then decides that this is as good as it's going to get. She watches one man row the boat into the little bay and keep the boat in place. The other man looks very much like a standard alien in his wetsuit and gear. Without the slightest noise he lowers himself overboard and disappears into the black water. Tiny ripples show that there must be someone underwater, while the other man looks around.

Martha doesn't dare to move, convinced the man will spot her in her high-up hiding place.

Time passes and soon Martha begins to feel like giving up – it all seems a bit odd spying on a man sitting in a boat. Then, the water heaves and sloshes, and the diver appears. In his hand he's carrying something. It's large, and he seems very careful. Martha is sure that it's one of the many amphorae, as she watches the man in the boat receive the artefact. The diver clambers into the little boat, and the two men bend over their find.

Martha keeps watching them, even when the diver goes down again, coming back with another item. She feels her anger growing. She very much enjoyed seeing the amphorae underwater and loved the shadow games with the sun – just to realise that those artefacts were very old and had been on the bottom of the sea in this gorgeous little cove for hundreds of years. Now these men are taking what doesn't belong to them, and the worst bit is that Martha can't do anything about it! For a few seconds she wonders whether she should overcome that fear as well, then dismisses it, for even she can see that it would be asking for very serious trouble. No, the right authorities will need to be informed. Ron will know what to do, and Martha feels a little thrill when she imagines herself tomorrow morning getting off the little boat, popping in to see Ron and casually telling him what she has found out. *"It's two men. One seems older."* She quickly smothers a giggle when the night vision goggles show his little goatie... The other one moves like a much younger man, but with all the gear and goggles there is no telling what he looks like.

She can just imagine Ron's stillness becoming even stiller, and his brown eyes looking at her, maybe slightly narrowed...

Martha swallows suddenly, not sure what she fears more, sitting here in the dark or telling Ron about it... *What if he thinks I was wrong? What if gets really angry, or even worse, what if it's his friends doing this and he's just the lookout?* Her hands are starting to shake, and she is suddenly quite sure that Ron will *not* be pleased. *Nobody will hear me or find me in those barracks,* she groans. *Imagine what he could do if he were really cross. He might feel he has to show me that this is his job, not mine, and he will "explain by demonstration", like William always said...*

The Voice seems nearer, and she can hear William's posh voice explaining that as she is obviously artistic, he will show her visually that he is unhappy with her decisions. *"After all, I am the head of the family, so I makes decisions. You decided to burn your favourite dress, after all..."* Martha gasps. She had forgotten... Not the visual demonstration, of course, but the fact that she was supposed to have burned her favourite dress. She had always believed him; but now, far away, she begins to doubt the incident. *After all, I hate fire. I wouldn't enjoy burning something. Definitely not my favourite dress either.* Over the Voice sounds another voice, a calm, controlled measured voice. *"Gaslighting, it's called,"* the cool voice says, and Martha pulls a face. She's not convinced that she can handle hearing Ron's voice in her daydreams...

She tries to concentrate on her job, needing to find out as much as she can. The night is still very dark, although the moon lights up the water. Martha trains the goggles on the men again; they seem to be talking in the little boat. The older man picks up the oars and rows off, and Martha puts the night goggles away carefully. She feels a little disappointed. *All that stress just for this? Two men in a little boat, one a diver, and then they go off again?* She leans back against the rough little trunk, suddenly very tired as well as cold. She snuggles down in her blanket and wobbles a little to get more comfortable. Then she half dozes off, not hearing any more of the two men. *They'll be home by now,* she thinks, feeling resentment against the two, as if they'd invited her to watch them.

Nearer the morning, close to dawn but while darkness is definitely still in charge, Martha yawns, stopping herself quickly. Under the blanket she carefully checks the time. "Good, it will be light quite soon," she says to herself. Another yawn makes her jaw give a funny click, and it reminds her again of those first days with her cracked jaw. Her throat is a bit dry, and she very quietly scrapes it, just as she thinks she hears something else.

She goes quiet, but no more is heard.

Martha sighs. *It's getting a bit boring now, just sitting here! I wish Anna and Dimitris came early.*

A definite sound can now be heard, and Martha tilts her head to one side in the hope that it will tell her more clearly where it came from. The moment she spots the coloured boat on the horizon, a strong, gloved hand forms round her throat, blocking all air from going in or out!

Martha gasps, and for a moment moves her hands as if to defend herself; then everything goes dark, and she slumps sideways, surprising her attacker.

A voice calls, and the man, after working on Martha for a few minutes, soundlessly slips back over rocks and through little ravines. No sound can be heard on the island, and in the pink sunlight sending pastel-coloured rays over the horizon, it all looks calm and peaceful.

24

ANNA WAKES UP TO DESPERATE RETCHING sounds from the small bathroom. She lies still in the dark, trying to make sense of the sounds, then groans. It's Dimitris. *That means he's got one of his violent migraines... which means... Oh no! No, not today, please Lord, not today of all days!*

Anna sits up in bed in horror, almost ready to join Dimitris in the bathroom. *No, I hate sailing the boat by myself...* She knows that if Dimitris has a migraine, he won't even be able to take the rubbish out, let alone the boat. That means that she, Anna, will have to take the boat out by herself to pick up Martha from the little island. Anna groans again, burying her face in her hands, feeling her stomach swirling along with each gasp. She loves the boat and is a very capable sailor, but ever since their dad was murdered Anna has been afraid to be by herself on it.

She can hear Dimitris staggering from the bathroom and can tell by the way he moves cautiously, bumping into doorframes, that his migraine has only just started. The fact that he bumps into the doorframes of both the bathroom and his own room tells her it's a bad one...

Anna lies down, staring in the dark towards her ceiling. She will have to take the boat and sail to Paximadi island, pick up Martha and come back. *That's all there is to it. Not a big deal,* she tells herself. *Not a big deal at all.*

"I give up," she mutters a little later. Sleep definitely won't come anymore, and by the time she gets to Paximadi it will be light. The robbers, if there are any, will be gone. Martha will be waiting at the little cove, no doubt anxious to be picked up. She will be able to spot the bright-coloured boat, and by the time Anna has sailed into the little cove, Martha will be ready. They will just sail back, then maybe have breakfast together, and she will drop Martha off at the resort. Life will be back to normal – well, *almost* normal. She will need to do the boat tour this afternoon, but Anna doesn't mind that; in fact, she enjoys talking to tourists, pointing out especially beautiful spots to them. No, she loves being out in the boat, provided *she isn't alone.* She sighs. This day is quite different from what she had envisaged, but by coffee time all will be fine. She gets up, dresses warmly, has a very quick breakfast and sets off towards the boat.

Anna shivers, not just from the cold early morning air, but from thoughts crowding in. "Fear not," she whispers, "I am with you always." She knows she's not alone, knows to put her trust in Christ, who is her Rock and Salvation. She thinks back to the day she heard about her father's death, the grief and despair, the overwhelming loneliness and futility of life. So many questions had come in, so much despair. A smile creeps onto her face; poor Pastor Volodya, she must have given him a full-time job just answering all her questions! He was a faithful man though, and answered all her questions and concerns, not once losing patience or interest, but showing genuine care and love for people. Her only regret is that it took a tragedy to bring her to Christ, having been closed to the gospel before.

Anna gets to the boat, scanning the horizon, hoping the sun will hurry up and just pop over the edge. She sighs, and slowly gets the boat ready. She knows she's not just scanning the horizon for the light; she is also checking for boats – boats with evil men, ready to kill people to avoid detection at all cost. The horizon is devoid of both though, and Anna sets off.

Being out on the smooth waters calms her, and the fact that there are no other boats to be seen comforts her. Soon she is almost enjoying the ride, especially as the sky is definitely starting to colour and light up. Paximadi can easily be seen now, and she feels relief creeping in. *Almost there. Let's hope Martha is waiting,* she thinks, a smile starting. *I wonder if she saw anything last night. I just hope she wasn't too scared.* She still can't believe that Martha actually came up with the plan to stay on the island overnight – Martha, who almost passed out by the idea of walking into church by herself, who is too shy to look at Dimitris properly, and who turns a funny colour whenever men or marriage is mentioned... *It's that Ron, even though she is very scared of him, it seems.* She grins, feeling curious about the man mentioned by Martha. *It's a shame I won't meet him, unless Martha has some really spectacular news, I suppose.* She dreams for a few minutes about meeting the guy with some interesting facts, lots of action following their news, and some worthwhile conversations...

Paximadi is now close by, and Anna starts straining her eyes every now and again, looking for the little cove, wondering if she will spot Martha on the rocky beach. No sign of life, no movement though – and Anna just sails on, carefully steering, taking her time. *It's very early, after all.*

Soon she can see the rocky beach, but still no sign of Martha. Tiny fingers start squeezing Anna's heart, icy fingers bringing fear. *Maybe she fell asleep,* she considers, *or maybe she hasn't looked this far out yet,* determined to find a reason for Martha's absence. *Maybe she's waiting till I'm closer, to avoid being seen.* There is no denying the fingers becoming colder and stronger though, and by the time Anna has stopped the boat, she is struggling to breathe.

There is definitely no sign of her friend. Her eyes scan the rocks, cracks, crevices… No movement, no sound, no Martha. She hesitates, then sounds the boat's horn. After a few moments she sounds the horn again, then waits. She keeps looking round, feeling uneasy, as well as worried about her friend's absence. *Where is she? She has to be close by, as this is the cove she wanted to watch…* There is no way Anna can leave the boat unattended, so she keeps staring at the grey rocks with tiny tufts of green sticking out around them. Her staring eyes become a little blurry from focussing on the island, and her thoughts drift to a painting she should make: the grey, the soft green, the blue underneath…

She sits back, her hand on the ship's wheel, wondering what to do. Sailing away feels like deserting her friend. She can't go onto the island to look for Martha – so what to do now? Dimitris is sick; he won't be able to come along with her on the boat. She bites her lip. *What now?* Then she thinks of the large man Martha mentioned and a plan forms quickly. *Yes, I'll go to the tiny harbour next to Sapphire Beach,* she decides, and starts the boat's engine.

Anna makes her way to the mainland rather quickly. She feels terrible leaving her friend behind. *What if Martha has had a fall?* She keeps looking back, hoping to see her appear on the beach after all. Then she looks ahead, hoping to spot the little harbour. Anna sighs. *I can't remember it being so far away!* She constantly prays for her friend's safety and wellbeing, and that she will understand why Anna had to go back…

Eventually, she spots the little harbour, relieved to find it empty. She knows some local people use the area to keep their small boats and can often be seen tinkering. Anna needs the harbour and beach to be deserted though; she must speak to Ron but doesn't want to betray his presence. She steers into the harbour carefully, struggling a little. She really doesn't like this part of sailing… She manages though, and ties up the boat, then walks towards the empty beach.

The sapphire blue sea makes it clear where the name came from. When Anna gets to the beach, she looks at the barracks across the road. *Which one is the barrack used by Ron?*

What do I do now, Lord? Just walk up to him? Wait here, or even call him? She hesitates. What if Ron isn't who he says he is… What if he has a terrible temper on him? After all, he doesn't know her; what if he feels threatened and attacks her? There is nobody around, so nobody will come looking for her here, will they? Anna swallows a few times, her mind busy between wondering and worrying on the one hand, and desperately praying for guidance on the other. Then she takes a deep breath, her decision made, and looks round carefully. After she has made sure there isn't a single person in sight, she crosses the road, and walks towards the barracks.

"Ron? Ron? Where are you? I'm Martha's friend. I need your help," she calls, trying to keep her voice down, as well as making it carry to reach Ron.

Movement catches her eyes, and Anna gasps. A large man appears in the door opening of one of the barracks. His whole body exudes strength and confidence. Not menacing, but definitely sending warning signals to whoever comes close. Anna walks up to him, trying to smile and walk as confidently as the man. "You are Ron? I'm Martha's friend. She told me about you, and I need your help," she says, feeling awfully demanding. It's only her fear for Martha's safety that is making her so forward, but Anna feels she has no choice. Ron hasn't moved, apart from that his eyes that narrowed just a little when Anna said that Martha had told her about him. Anna is closer now, and says, "Martha is on the little island. She wanted to see if thieves would come in the night. We were going to pick her up this morning, but she isn't there. I mean, she didn't come to the beach. I couldn't leave the boat, but she might have fallen or something. My brother is ill; he couldn't come. I didn't want anyone else to know. I mean, my brother doesn't know about you, he just thought…" She stops. *The guy won't be interested in all that, will he?* Anna keeps looking straight at Ron and sees the surprise in his eyes, then worry.

"She's on Paximadi?" he asks, his cool voice sounding quite incredulous.

Anna nods, and smiles a little. If she hadn't dropped Martha off herself, she wouldn't have believed it either.

"She's been there all night?"

Yes, he's definitely incredulous. Anna smiles a bit more. *I'll tell Martha how I managed to really shock the guy; that will please her!*

Ron nods. "I'll get my bag," he says, turning and walking into the dark barrack.

Anna is a little worried when he reappears within seconds, walking quickly. She realises that he must be worried to move at that speed. They walk to the boat without saying anything, and he helps her with the ropes.

Anna feels a little nervous – she hates people watching her steer the boat – but Ron doesn't seem to notice. He is looking through his binoculars, scanning both Dia and Paximadi. Soon the little cove appears, but still no Martha. Anna sighs, feeling tears sting her eyes. She was so sure that Martha would be on the beach this time, anxiously waiting for them. Somehow this time round it's worse, and she quickly swipes her tears away.

"No worries; she's probably fallen asleep, that's all," the calm voice says, making Anna jump as well as blush. "You're right, maybe she has fallen somewhere and hurt her ankle or something. We'll soon find her."

Anna nods, because she can tell from the way Ron talks that he expects her to go along with his explanations. Anna is not convinced though; the icy fingers still hold her heart in their arctic grip.

25

ANNA WATCHES RON LOWER HIMSELF INTO the water, swimming to the rocky beach with strong, confident strokes, holding his rucksack with one hand. She smiles a little, for the contrast between Martha and Ron couldn't be bigger! *No wonder Martha shivered every time she talked about Ron!* Anna feels intimidated herself, and just prays that Ron is really one of the good guys... She watches him get out of the water, shake himself a little dry, his shorts dripping, then puts socks and army boots back on. He shrugs the rucksack on, and gives her a short wave before setting off, following the track where Anna said Martha went the day before.

Anna just waits, feeling anxious, still scanning the water and the rest of the tiny island. Something feels wrong; it's as if even the air is too quiet. *If only Dimitris had been well enough to come,* she thinks, then blushes. Surely someone like Ron will be better at finding Martha than she is. In fact, if Martha has hurt her leg, Ron could just carry her back. The image of Ron carrying Martha makes her giggle, then she turns serious again. *What if he doesn't find her? What if those thieves found her first, and did to Martha what they did to my father?* Anna bites her lip, praying for her friend, praying for herself, that she will be able to handle whatever Ron finds.

Ron is out of sight for a long time, and Anna can feel the tension growing in her heart. She tries singing to herself softly, just to remind herself that God is in control. When she notices how her voice trembles, she pulls a face and stops, feeling that soon tears will clog up her throat. Then, just when she decides that she can't wait any longer without doing something – *anything* – Ron appears from behind a rock. Alone.

Anna's heart sinks and her dark eyes fill with tears. *No Martha!* Ron has come back without Martha, looking calm but serious. Anna doesn't hesitate, but quickly strips off her clothes and dives into the water, grateful that she did wear her swimsuit after all. She swims to the shore as fast as she can, unable to wait any longer. Something must have happened, and the boat doesn't seem important all of a sudden. She reaches the rocky beach and wipes the water off her face, looking at Ron, searching his face to see what the bad news is. Ron nods at Anna, waiting for her to catch her breath.

"I didn't see Martha. I found these though," he says, and from the pocket of his trunks he pulls bits of rope, cut in two.

Anna gasps, and looks back at him. "What does that mean? Was Martha found and tied up? Then why is the rope cut, and where is she now? Did they come back for her, free her from the ropes, and take her with them?" Anna's eyes fill with sudden tears.

Ron shakes his head, his cool voice slower and less clipped than usual. "We don't know. The rope hasn't been there long, definitely not even a few days. We don't know if it had anything to do with Martha, and we don't know if she's in trouble at the moment."

Anna just cries quietly, overcome with guilt. "I should have looked for her this morning," she sobs. "I knew something was wrong. I just didn't want to leave the boat. I worried that the thieves might take it and we'd both be stranded. I just wish I had made Martha my priority. I'm so sorry!"

Ron looks uneasy, clearly unsure what to say to make things better or how to stop Anna's tears.

Anna does stop after a while though, knowing that tears won't help them just now. She wipes her face, looks at Ron, and blushes a little when she sees his uneasiness. "Sorry," she says, her voice only wobbling a little. "What do we do now?"

Ron shrugs a little, looking round the cove.

"Did you search the rest of the island?" Anna asks, and he shakes his head, saying he came back once he found the rope. He wanted to explain to Anna what he had found. Anna thinks about the island and its shape for a moment. *Maybe she is still on the island, but in a different hiding place?* She knows the chances are slim; after all, how would Martha manage to cut the rope, and why would she hide somewhere else, knowing that Anna was coming? On the other hand, maybe she had woken up when Anna was already leaving the island. In that case, she might have wanted to hide somewhere. Anna sighs, feeling overwhelmed, afraid that they will move past Martha at this rate, and come back empty-handed.

"Do you know the island?" Ron's voice sounds calm, practical, and Anna is sure that he looks relieved to see her less emotional. She nods, explaining that she often went with her brother, and how she has explored the tiny island.

Ron nods, and Anna feels annoyed with herself for again giving him a lot of surplus information. *Not sure whether Martha and I have improved his opinion of women. I give too much information and cry; Martha more or less passed out on him... Great...* She forces herself to think straight and starts describing the tiny island to Ron, who listens intently, making Anna squirm inside.

"It's basically just rock," explains Anna. "There are a few cracks though, and some caves, although they're usually underwater ones. It's hard to hide on this island."

Ron nods, and says he found the rope near the trunk of a windswept bush, which seemed to be the only living thing on the island.

Anna nods. "It's impossible for anything to grow here; it's so rocky and windswept! It's the water that attracts the tourists – and seeing the artefacts underwater. Some of them like swimming into the coves as well."

Ron nods to show he understands. "I will have a quick walk round the island," he says. "I don't want to call her name, as she might not recognise my voice." He looks a little awkward then, but when he sees Anna smiling with understanding, he grins his lopsided smile at her. "If she is in a tricky situation, I don't want her to panic, thinking there is a man after her," he says, then looks serious again. "I really don't know what happened. The rope looks cut, but not with a very clean cut, so it seems that whoever was tied up cut themself free. I don't know if Martha had a knife on her?"

Anna shrugs her shoulders, then admits that she doesn't know very much about Martha's past, only that men don't seem to be her favourite...

Ron chuckles at that and simply says, "Her ex-husband was abusive."

Anna nods, and thinks out loud that Martha might well have had a knife in that case... "She expected the thieves to be men, or at least for there to be one thief. With that sort of background, she might have felt that a knife could be useful, even if just to give her more confidence."

Ron nods.

"I'll wait here," she says when she sees Ron getting ready.

As soon as he is out of sight, Anna regrets her choice. The island that is usually so beautiful and sweet now feels dark and menacing, in spite of the bright sun overhead and the wonderful blue waters around her. She feels warm, but in spite of the late morning heat, Anna shivers. "Where are you, Martha?" she whispers, feeling the tears stinging again. "What has happened to you? Have the men found you and taken you?"

Anna waits, listening for noises, listening for Ron's return. It's very quiet, and after a while she finds that she just can't stand it anymore. She starts swimming around the little cove, watching the amphorae underneath, smiling at the little fish, her mind going round and round in circles. Anna follows the cove to the jutting out rocks, and turns round. By the time Ron reappears, she has been up and down the cove many times, somehow soothed by the movement and the exercise. She can tell from Ron's face that he hasn't found Martha, and she bites her lip, fighting the tears. She really doesn't want to cry again, *but what now?*

They get to the little rocky beach at the same time, and Anna just looks at Ron, mute. He shrugs his shoulder, his eyes looking serious, and Anna loses the fight against new tears...

"Would Martha know about the underwater caves and how easy are they to get to?" he asks when Anna finally manages to dry her eyes.

She nods, explaining that there are several of them, one in this cove, which she has looked in already.

Ron thinks, then wonders aloud whether Martha could have cut the rope, then gone down into one of the underwater caves.

Anna nods, more because she wants it to be true than that she really thinks Martha would have done so.

"Where is the next cave after this one?" Ron asks, his eyes scanning the water, the coastline and the rocks around them.

Anna bites her lip; she is sure that Ron can feel the tension in the air as well. She points to the jutting-out rock and explains that if you go past it, soon you will come to another cave. She offers to go, as she is wet already, and Ron hesitates. Then he shakes his head.

"I'll go, just in case Martha has hurt herself, and you never know..." He stops, and Anna feels herself going pale.

I know, she thinks. *He means, you never know who is with her, or who else is hiding, or in what sort of condition she is...* So she just agrees, watching him walk towards the rock with confident strides, scaling the rock as easy as the kri-kri do. She waits till he has gone out of sight, then cries again, overwhelmed with grief for her friend, sure that Martha has come to grief.

This doesn't improve when Ron comes swimming round the rock, his muscled arms ploughing through the water with ease, holding something in his hand. He gets to Anna, who tries to smile, having dried her face, hoping he won't notice her red eyes... "Do you recognise this?" he asks. "I found it just at the mouth of the cave."

Anna feels the world spinning and opens her mouth to answer, but no sound comes out. She gasps when an iron hand clamps round her arm to steady her.

"That's Martha's sandal, isn't it?" Ron asks, and Anna nods. Ron looks a little pleased, and says, "In which case she is probably in that cave," and looks at Anna. "Shall I go in, or do you think it's better for you to go?"

Anna thinks about it. She'd love to do something to help her friend. She still feels guilty for letting her down by sailing away. *On the other hand, what if Martha is not alone...?*

Ron smiles his unique smile and says, "I'll be right behind you. I'll wait at the rock, so she won't be able to see me. If you call me, I will hear you and be there in seconds. Alright?"

Anna is relieved, and together they swim to the rock, Anna exerting herself, Ron keeping up with the greatest of ease... When they get to the rock, he stops and winks at her.

Anna blushes, feeling annoyed with herself for it, and swims on, biting her lip, not swimming so fast now. Slowly she swims into the shadows of the overhanging rocks. There she hesitates, then whispers loudly, "Martha? Martha, are you there? It's Anna... Are you there, Martha?"

26

MARTHA SHAKES AND SHIVERS, HER STOMACH empty, and not just because of a lack of breakfast. She hides at the back of the cave, in the darkest spot, the water cool, rocks smooth and black as the pit of despair. Her breathing sounds loud in her ear, whooshing and hissing, and her eyes are as black as her surroundings. Her hands are shaking too much to tuck her hair behind her ear, and in a way, her terror is too great for such a small movement.

Martha groans and whimpers, cowering further and further into the rock, her eyes staring at the entrance and the tiny slither of light where she came in, never once moving from there, unblinking. "I'm a… a…" Her lips hardly move, her tongue uncooperative, and as her mind is unable to remember what she was meant to be saying, the words stay locked in, in fear. "No, I'm not a…" That doesn't lead to anything either, and Martha is too cold and too scared to allow the slightest bit of energy to be diverted to her mind to finish her thoughts. Her brain screams that it could be something important – but not now. Her heart is too busy pumping blood at a ridiculously high rate around her body and has no time for feelings and mantras.

With everything in her body on overdrive, even that isn't quite enough to deal with the terror. Every now and then, Martha's eyes roll back, her knees buckle a little, but as soon as her lips taste the salty water, her mind recovers enough to straighten recalcitrant limbs and focus her eyes enough to pin themselves on the cave entrance again.

Martha has absolutely no idea how long she has been here or even why she is here. She has some fleeting images, but her whole system is in panic mode, so all thoughts of why and how are blocked – until a dark shadow slides into the little slither of light. Martha freezes up completely, her breathing stops, and for a second it seems her heart does too, only to double its speed. An urgent whisper echoes round the dark cave. "Martha? Are you there? It's Anna, it's me. Martha…?"

Martha gasps, the shaking increases and her legs give way. She falls into the water properly, just gasping, choking, struggling, her whole body convulsing out of sheer horror.

"Martha!" The voice sounds desperately worried, and a slim body swims over to her as fast as possible. "Martha, you're here! I'm so…" The voice stops, for to say that you're glad when someone is beyond petrified might be the wrong choice of words… Anna soon reaches Martha, holding her up, tears in her eyes, for she can tell that she is in a bad shape. "Shhh, it's alright, my friend," she whispers, her voice calm, soothing, holding on to the shaking woman. "It's alright, you're perfectly safe now, it's alright." Anna can feel herself shivering in sympathy and cold, and knows that going out of the cave into the warmth is important. *How will Martha react when she sees Ron, though?* "Listen, Martha," she says urgently.

"Listen, we need to get out of the cave, into the warmth, alright? Outside the cave is Ron – you remember Ron? I asked him to help me. Dimitris is ill. Ron is outside the cave, alright? Let's go."

Martha nods but makes no movement at all. Anna tries to slowly move towards the cave mouth, but Martha is shaking too much. In the end Anna has to give up. She hesitates, then calls softly, "Ron? Ron, Martha is here, but I could do with a hand!"

Again, the thin strip of lights is broken up for a moment, and a much larger shape swims into the cave. Ron's eyes narrow a little when he sees the state that Martha is in, but he doesn't say anything. He quietly moves next to Anna, just behind Martha, and gently takes hold of Martha's upper arm. As soon as she feels his grip, her breathing speeds up and turns into fast, desperate gasps. Ron doesn't let go, but slowly moves her towards the mouth of the cave. She whimpers and half struggles, but Ron carries on the trek without saying a word.

Anna's eyes are filled with tears, to see her friend like this! Poor Martha, what has happened to her?

Once they're out of the cave, Martha turns towards Ron, terror splattered over her face, but his calm voice stops her. "It's alright, Martha, Anna is just behind you," he says, pointing towards Anna with his chin. "You're perfectly safe now; we're here to help you."

Martha stares at him wildly for just a few seconds, then breaks out into hysterical sobs. Ron only blinks fast a few times, then holds her tightly. Anna is busily scrubbing her own eyes, but somehow manages to smile at his restraint!

Ron holds Martha, his cool voice slower and softer than usual, and if Martha had been able to look, she would have noticed the absence of his curled lip. He isn't laughing at her or looking down at her in any way. His eyes never rest though, and Anna finds herself looking at the water and the rocks as well. The odd feeling is still there, and she can't wait to get into the boat.

After a while Martha seems to calm down a little, and Ron sets her back from himself a few inches. He looks at her, his voice warmer than either of the women have ever heard. "Alright? Now, let's get you into the boat, shall we? Any idea where your bag might be?"

This makes Anna look around the mouth of the cave even more, and suddenly she spots a coloured bit of cloth between some rocks. She swims across and sighs with relief. The bag! By standing on a few rocks she manages to pull the bag free, as well as Martha's clothes pushed under it, and swims behind Ron and Martha, keeping Martha's things above water.

Ron lifts Martha with one arm while climbing the little ladder onto the boat with the other. Anna pulls a face, wishing she could take a picture to show Dimitris... He and his friends are very competitive, always talking about the biggest fish, the longest time rowing, the longest dive underwater, the heaviest rope or box... *Now, to carry a woman with one arm up a ladder – that's something to brag about,* Anna giggles to herself, relief growing that Martha has been found. She hurts for her friend though, and she feels her stomach churning when she remembers Martha's fear when first found.

Once Martha is on the boat, Anna pulls the towel from her bag, drying her a little before tucking the blanket around her. It's hot on deck, but Martha is shaking as if she's been rescued from under the ice, instead of a cave in the Mediterranean! Anna watches her friend, her own eyes stinging, her nose runny, but slowly warming up in the sun. Ron has dried himself as well, and just stands nearby, still on his guard though, and Anna suddenly wants to go. Away from this island, away from the menacing feelings in the air.

With one last look at Martha she turns to Ron. "Shall we go? Where do you want to go? Back to the little harbour near Sapphire Beach?"

Ron thinks for a few seconds, his eyes scanning the rocks, then agrees.

Anna is relieved, and quickly looks over the boat, pulling in the little anchor she used, checking the last few things, taking a few sips of lukewarm water, then starts the engine. She feels a surge of relief when the engine starts, purring as usual; somehow, because of Martha's fear, Anna doubted a smooth getaway. She steers into the open sea, feeling relief in leaving Paximadi. It feels as if they're getting out from under a dark cloud as well, and Anna starts singing to herself again. This time the hymns are more upbeat, and she can feel her body and soul relaxing together.

Ron studies Martha, and when she looks up, he smiles his lopsided grin at her. He sees the corners of her mouth moving, but the fear is still too powerful to allow for a smile. Martha can see him through swollen blurred-vision eyes. She sees the calm face, remembers the cool, soft voice telling her everything would be alright, and she suddenly realises that she actually believed him. Yes, it would be alright. She has no idea why Ron is here on the boat with

190

Anna, no idea where Dimitris is, no idea why she is so cold. She isn't even quite sure why she is shaking so much and why her throat aches from her gasping breaths. Ron said it would be alright, and his voice strengthened the other voice in her head – the one that had been trying to get through, the one that kept whispering, "Fear not." It had been such a sweet voice that she had totally disregarded it. Now that voice is louder, and somehow has a Ukrainian accent...

Martha drops her head on her arms. *That went well,* she groans inside. *'Fear not' – and when Ron finds me I'm going insane with fear. He will be so angry for having to look for me, and just for having to come out.* The shakes begin again, and soft sobs start their rhythm all afresh. She can sense him sitting down next to her, and Martha gulps in air, fighting to at least stop the crying, to try to explain, to... to do anything to take the edge off Ron's anger...

"Martha, it's alright," the calm voice says. "We found you. You're on Anna's boat; we'll get you all sorted out. Are you hurt anywhere as far as you know?" Ron had given her a quick look over once on the boat but had seen no blood anywhere. He noticed a few red lines on her wrists and guessed that cutting off the rope hadn't been as easy as it sounds.

Martha sits quietly, processing his words, then shakes her head.

"Would you like a drink?" Ron asks, opening a bottle of water anyway, and when Martha slowly lifts her head, he hands her the open bottle, waiting to make sure that her shaking hand has a good grip. She takes a few sips, swallowing hard, then glances at him.

He grins and says, "You found a good place to hide – just a bit cold," making her smile a tiny bit. "I found your sandal, so Anna went to have a look. Dimitris is not well." Then, when he sees the worry flare up in her eyes, he quickly explains, "He woke up with a migraine, apparently, so Anna came by herself. Did you see Anna arriving at the island earlier this morning?"

Martha pinches her lips together to stop herself from crying and nods, her memory returning. She shivers, and she isn't sure how happy she is with returning memories, desperate to forget these last few hours.

27

MARTHA OPENS HER MOUTH, BUT HER DEEP breath doesn't feed her oxygen, it just makes terror flood in again, constricting her stomach, making her heart speed up erratically. She pulls her knees up tighter towards her chest, squeezes her eyes shut to close out her fear, and moans, shaking and sobbing softly.

Ron looks concerned, as well as determined, and Anna doesn't know whether he will step in or not. He doesn't; he just sits quietly, very still, waiting for Martha.

Anna sighs. *Poor Martha! She looks absolutely terrified. She saw me and obviously saw me sailing away as well...* She feels horror growing inside her as she watches her friend. *No wonder she is terrified! How awful! I wonder what happened afterwards... Was she already tied up, or was that rope not connected?* She looks at Ron, admiring his patience. Martha seems to just retreat further and further, scaring Anna. *What if Martha slips into proper shock? What if she was hurt, after all?* Anna bites her lip, and when she makes eye contact with Ron, she whispers, "Should we take her to a doctor? Our doctor is very good and..." But Martha has heard, and sits up, wide-eyed, her hand over her mouth.

"No! No! I will not see a doctor. I'm not going anywhere near a doctor. I won't..." She is shaking so much, the words won't come out anymore. She pushes the blanket off as much as possible and starts crawling to the side of the boat, clearly with the idea of getting off the vessel!

Ron just leans forward on one knee and his large hand takes hold of Martha's upper arm. Anna squirms, feeling for her friend. *When you're this terrified already, to have a big guy grab your arm?*

Martha struggles and whimpers, but Ron won't budge. His grip is careful, gentle, but very firm, and it's not going anywhere.

"I'm not seeing a doctor," Martha stutters, trying in vain to push away from Ron. Soon she is too exhausted to fight, and she just moves her feet in a token effort to get away, her breath coming in sobbing loud gasps.

Ron has stayed quiet, probably because he knows that a male voice at this time will not be very helpful. "Martha, you will be alright," he says finally, his voice lower than usual, "just sit back and let's put that blanket back on you so you will stay warm. No one will force you to see a doctor. However, we thought of a doctor as you seemed to be pulling back further and further and started slipping into shock." He looks at Martha as if daring her to argue this point, but she doesn't; she merely shakes her head.

Anna's eyes are stinging with tears. She just wishes she could help her friend. Even she finds Ron rather intimidating, if not frightening, so how he will come across to Martha with her background, she can only imagine.

"Martha, you will need to work with us in that case," Ron says, his voice almost back to the usual cool, clipped sound. "We need to know if you're hurt, if you saw

194

anything, if you need anything. Going into shock or major breakdown is something that Anna and I cannot help you with. It would also be irresponsible of us if we left you in a very bad state. You understand, don't you?" As he looks at Martha, Anna spots the tension in his jaw, and it relieves her. He feels for her, she realises; he really feels for her, and is not some hardnosed guy who looks down on her.

The boat goes very quiet. Ron just looks at Martha, and Anna is praying and willing Martha to answer, to speak up, to allow them to help her. Martha sits hugging the blanket, shivering, a thin finger peeking out from the blanket to push her glasses up higher and to tuck her hair behind her ear. Anna smiles a little, hoping that those are signs that she is getting there!

Martha finally whispers, "Yes, I saw Anna. I was so relieved." She stops, her lips moving without any sound, trying to catch her breath.

Ron just sits quietly, his eyes intent and focussed. Anna bites her lips, her own eyes filling in sympathy.

Martha takes another deeper breath and continues. "Just as I spotted her, somebody grabbed my throat and throttled me. I... I passed out. And when I came round I was tied to the little tree and Anna was just leaving the cove." Tears come faster then, and renewed shakes. "I... went out again, I suppose, and the next time I came round I heard them whisper about 'Not now, later,' sorting things out and whatnot... and then quiet. I knew" – Martha sobs, feeling the sheer terror flooding in again – "I knew I had to get away as soon as I could. I had packed a kitchen knife in my bag, but it was so hard!"

Ron purses his lips and gives a chuckle. "Yes, getting a knife from a bag to get yourself free... Impossible, really!"

Martha lifts her chin and a tiny sparkle of humour, even confidence, appears. "Well, my sister and I used to play games like that, so I kicked off my sandals and set to work! I was always pretty good at it, I must admit," she says, with mock humility, making Ron laugh – a sudden explosive "Ha!" which in turn makes both women giggle.

Ron rolls his eyes, leaning back with a mock sigh.

Then Martha says, "I was determined. I knew I was going to be sick, or pass out for the third time, or just cry and scream, so I... I *prayed* and, well, apologised for my crazy plan, but eventually I got the knife out of the bag. It was really hard to get it to my hands and I almost gave up." Martha goes quiet, wondering what would have happened to her had she done so, hating the remembering, wishing she could just move on, not think about those sinister voices. "The rope gave way, I got my stuff together, and went towards the little cove when I'm sure I heard the men. There was nowhere to hide, so I ran, then saw the smaller cave that was mentioned and decided to try and hide there. I stuffed my bag under a rock with my clothes and got into the water. The cave opening looked so dark and scary, but I heard one of the men give a shout, and I knew they had realised I was gone." Martha feels her stomach turning, remembering the man's angry exclamation. "So I went in but I stayed near the entrance for a bit; it was so dark and cold. I heard the boat, but thought it was the men searching the coastline, so I went in the back of the cave, and... and I was just so scared," she ends, her voice shaking, feeling weak and feeble for going to pieces like that; wondering whether Ron will get angry in front of Anna, or whether he will leave that for another day; wondering if it will be enough to keep the doctor away.

Ron nods, looking over to the tiny island they have left behind, looking picturesque in the midday sunshine. "Thanks, Martha! Well done for getting free. That was impressive," he smiles, and then his face grows serious again. "Do you think they might be the thieves?"

Martha nods, and explains that she saw two men in the night, wrinkling her nose as she explains about the older man with the goatie.

Ron looks at her, and she giggles suddenly, explaining the image she had had in her head of the rogue archaeologist, complete with goatie, socks and sandals.

"Did he have socks and sandals?" Ron asks, and they share a laugh, all three feeling lighter now Martha is speaking and her intense fear seems to be trickling away.

Martha tries to describe it all as well as she can, and she feels bad when she can't really describe the diver.

"No worries; you did very well," Ron assures her, his eyes drifting a bit, and Martha knows he is planning his next move. At least, that is what she hopes he is doing and not plotting out some punishment for her seeing that she gave him incomplete information.

"You did really well," agrees Anna, smiling at Martha. "I'm not sure that I could have watched those men without getting into a panic! And to have to watch my boat disappear this morning... I would have been frantic! You did *very* well." Anna nods as if someone is going to debate the point with her.

Martha blushes and looks less grey, and Ron grins. He agrees with Anna, but still wonders what on earth Martha was thinking… He almost opens his mouth, but before he can even ask her, Anna looks at him with such a pleading look that he caves in. After all, it's not going to change anything by questioning Martha's sound judgment now, is it?

Martha blushes even more, her eyes staring at the edge of the blanket, her fingers twisting the blanket this way and that, before she answers. "The pastor, Pastor Volodya, had been preaching about overcoming your fears, not giving in to them, and to trust God in difficult situations. I had allowed fear to take over in my marriage. I was so afraid of William that even when I realised what he did was wrong, I kept quiet. I wanted him to be right, and I didn't want the long battles over what really happened, so I always allowed him to explain what happened. I even let myself believe his version of events, rather than have the courage to stand up to him. In the end I couldn't recognise truth if it hit me in the face!"

Ron looks serious but doesn't say anything.

"Then when Pastor Volodya said all that, I felt guilty and convicted because I know I didn't trust God with the outcome, I didn't trust God to keep me safe. In a way I wanted a retake, another chance to prove that I could be brave and… and trust God."

Ron frowns a little, his eyes very slightly narrowed. "Are you sure that your pastor had this sort of thing in mind?"

Martha pulls a face, trying to look annoyed but failing, and she sighs with an embarrassed laugh. "No, when I saw the men, I suddenly realised that God might have wanted me to be brave and do the right thing in *my own* situation. He didn't ask or expect me to go and search for dangerous criminals by myself on some weird rock off the coast of Crete in the middle of the night."

Ron laughs.

"By then it was too late, of course, and I was so scared! When morning came and Anna's boat appeared, I was so relieved that God had kept me safe through the night and that my crazy plan was finally over, and then…" The feel of the man's hand round her throat is there instantly, making Martha lightheaded in the same moment. Warm, hard fingers on her shoulder bring her back down immediately though, and she manages a smile almost as lopsided and wonky as Ron's, relieved as well as slightly afraid of his ability to read her mind.

28

ANNA STEERS THE COLOURFUL BOAT INTO THE little harbour, looking like a little boat on a pleasure trip. She's feeling anything but pleasure though, just relief that they reached the harbour. Ron, still looking around and shielding his eyes against the bright sun, jumps onto the concrete, tying the boat up securely. Martha looks much better, the colour back in her thin face. Ron helps her out of the boat, and she lets him, surprised at herself. Somehow his strong hands give her a sense of security, and she smothers all thoughts of those hands hitting or pushing her away. Anna looks more like her smiley self, pleased that they're back in the little harbour. She felt vulnerable out on the water, images of her dad's lifeless body coming to mind far too often. Ron looks tense, and Martha can't help looking over her shoulder all the time, the sunny beach and wonderful blue water an odd contrast to the fear and danger that lie behind them. They settle down on the hot beach, and Ron looks at the two young women, his face serious.

"You did well in getting away and hiding, Martha," he begins, and Martha feels a little shiver of apprehension, guessing that the 'but' will come, wondering if he will just threaten her, or whether he'll let her off the hook. "Next time you might not be so lucky though, so please, leave it to others, alright?" He smiles at her with his lopsided grin and his eyes stay soft. No fury or anger at all are to be seen in them, and Martha feels a funny sensation deep in her stomach. She messed up – *really* messed up – and the guy isn't in the least bit angry? "Please stay near the hotel. Don't go to Iraklion by yourself. This beach should be alright, church and things with others is fine as well. I just want to make sure that they won't find out who it was that saw them. The boat is pretty big, after all."

He stops when he sees both women turn pale, and Anna puts her hand over her mouth, her eyes wide with fear.

"It's a precaution, nothing else," he shrugs, trying to sound casual, but Martha notices that he doesn't take his words back either. "Just be extra careful, and don't go out by yourself. After all, the man that tied you up will have seen your face, so he might check around. It's wise to be careful." He smiles at Martha, clearly trying to make it sound better than it does, and she can feel her hands beginning to shake, her wrists aching now that the shock of the whole ordeal has worn off a little. Funnily enough, she feels hungry as well! "I will get in touch with some of my friends and we'll take it from there. Does Dimitris have another boat, like a small motorboat of some sort?"

He turns to Anna and she shakes her head, explaining that they use the boat of one of his friends when they need to.

"Does he let others use it?" Ron is clearly planning the next few steps; Martha can just see him forming lists in his head. *No need for a Lifeline there,* she sighs to herself.

"I'm sure you can borrow it," Anna smiles bravely, still shaken by his words. The idea that somebody watched them sail away and recognised their boat makes her feel ill. What if they find out the name of the boat, the owner of the boat? They didn't see the men anywhere, but that doesn't mean that the men weren't watching them. How much would they have been able to see from Dia? Not much, probably, if anything. Maybe they had just been at sea, just outside their view, with a good strong pair of binoculars… "Will it be safe for Dimitris to go to Paximadi with the boat next time?" she asks, although he hasn't had any bookings for the day trip yet.

Ron thinks for a moment, his eyes scanning the blue sea, so calm and peaceful. Then he nods, and explains that in the daytime, with holidaymakers around, it should be perfectly safe.

"I know he hasn't got any trips booked, but even so," Anna explains, biting her lips. "How do I contact you about that little boat? Do you want me to ask our friends on your behalf?" She looks at Ron, hoping he won't find her too pushy.

He hesitates, then asks for both their phones. He taps away at the screens, adding himself to their contacts. "Text me if you see anything, hear anything," he says, and Martha looks up at the sense of urgency in his voice. "Anna, if you could have a word with your friends, that would be great," he says, adding himself to Martha's contacts. "Martha, I would like you to leave Anna's number with the reception in the resort, if Anna is alright with that. It's better to have a local contact number with all this going on."

His voice sounds very reasonable and relaxed, but Martha feels her shoulders tensing up. *Why would he ask me to do that if he doesn't expect any trouble? Does he*

know something about these two men that we don't?
Could it be that his background has made him extra
careful, paranoid even? Or hasn't he told us everything
about the thieves? She can feel the shakes setting in as she
wonders about last night. *Was I in even greater danger*
than I thought?

Again, Ron seems to guess the reason that her hands
are shaking. "It's just to be safe, Martha. It's always good
to cover all your bases. I'm not expecting anything to
happen. I'm just saying that it's possible, and in that case
it's good to have a contact number available. If you do see
anyone with socks, sandals and a goatie" – he grins
suddenly – "then contact me straightaway and stay out of
the guy's sight!"

Martha has to smile when he mentions the man's
particulars, blushing that he remembers the socks and
sandals bit, then laughing a little when she thinks of the
many Brits she has seen this holiday wearing socks and
sandals. No goatie though…

Anna walks Martha back to the resort to have a simple
lunch together. Martha is hungrier than she has been for
ages. She is relieved to have Anna with her though because
she feels suddenly very vulnerable. Ron's strong presence
somehow made her feel safe, even though his looks make
her heart beat fast with panic lurking in the corners. She
remembers the grip on her arm and how she was unable
to move an inch, but funnily enough, the memory doesn't
have the same edge as the times that William gripped her
arms. Those memories are enough to make her shake, or
even feel sick, whereas the moments on the boat where
Ron prevented her from jumping ship seem fine.
Absentmindedly she rubs her arms, then forces herself

away from those thoughts. She has a sense that if she studies the contrast between these feelings, she might end up on dangerous ground! She looks back towards the golden beach, the sun making the sand glow and the sapphire water sparkle. Ron has disappeared into the barracks again, softly talking into his phone, his face tight, hard and focussed.

Over lunch Martha feels herself relaxing a little and she finds herself talking about England and the Cotswolds without the usual anxiety. *It actually feels quite like talking about home,* she realises. "I was hurting so much, and so scared all the time, blaming myself, but deep down blaming him for making me feel too scared to do the right thing," she explains to Anna. "I blamed him for taking my art away, even though that was my decision – I was too scared to get pencils and draw again. I have let fear rule me for far too long, and to be honest, I don't really know how to change that. Last night was a foolish attempt to prove that I wasn't afraid, and I'm glad God helped me out of the hole I got myself into!"

Anna nods, her eyes filling with tears when she remembers the state Martha was in when she found her.

"Also, I blamed God for not giving me the strength I needed to do the right thing, so when Pastor Volodya preached about it, I just really struggled."

Together they walk to reception after lunch, and Martha leaves Anna's name and number there.

"Just in case," she smiles at the girl, trying to make it look a normal thing to do as a holiday rep. The girl smiles back and puts the little note somewhere safe; at least, Martha *hopes* it's safe, and prays that it will never be needed. She still shudders, hearing Ron's serious voice, seeing his tight face...

Martha has a nap just before dinner and works on a new drawing in the evening. She positions the new paper, gets out her pencils, then sits there, her fingers lightly tracing the paper. She blushes a little, her hands not as steady as usual when she finally starts drawing, but she excuses this by reminding herself how tired she is and how much she has been through. The outline on paper is just right though – a strong, manly face, short hair, set chin. Martha finds herself smiling a little, then her smile becomes a concentrated frown as she works on a lopsided grin, realising how hard it is to get it just so. Cicadas chirp in the background, and even though Martha has spent all afternoon looking over her shoulder, an uneasy feeling in her shoulders, her eyes never leave the paper.

By the time it gets too dark to work comfortably, Martha leans back with a satisfied sigh, her stomach twisting a little with an unaccustomed feeling, but it's one that makes her feel... happy. Her hand hovers over the page of her 'blessing journal', wondering if she should put it down in writing. In the end she manages to keep it neutral enough. "Ron and Anna got me safely back." She hesitates, then smiles and puts her journal away. Martha decides to fill in her gaudy notebook in the morning, too exhausted to relive the night and day's terrors just now.

29

ANNA LOOKS AROUND THE SHOP, A SWEET smile shaping her mouth upwards. She loves the smell of paint, paper and pencils, and whichever corner she looks at, there are colours, neatly blended together. She sighs, her mind drifting back to yesterday, relieved that Dimitris was so much better today and able to take the boat out himself. Anna told him a little of what had happened, trying to keep Ron out of the picture. Dimitris looked completely lost as she related what had happened, and to be honest, she got a little lost in the retelling herself! All she wanted him to know what that Paximadi was off limits for now and that Dimitris should keep his eyes open and stay out of trouble…

Dimitris looked as if he were going to ask a lot of awkward questions, but in the end, he just rubbed his temples, groaned and explained that his head was still too fuzzy to deal with it all. "I'm sure there is a lot more to all this, but for now I'm going to rest, and sort the boat out later," he said, his voice dull and flat, as it always was once his migraine was on the way out.

Anna shudders a little, grateful that it all ended the way it did, praying that nothing will happen and that Ron and his friends will sort it all out. She wonders vaguely how he will do that. *It's a shame, in a way, as it will mean him leaving the area, no doubt. Mind you, he is a little intimidating.* She smiles a bit, then mumbles, "Probably a good thing he's going."

Just then her phone rings, a Cretan number, and Anna answers it with the fast, musical Cretan greeting. However, the sales assistant smile that automatically accompanies the cheerful "Parakalo" dies off as soon as she hears the young girl's voice on the other end. The voice sounds a little accusing, questioning Anna. Her hand travels to her mouth at the same speed as the girl's words. She shakes her head, knowing the girl can't see that, and when she stops, Anna explains that, no, she has no idea, and yes, she'll try and find out, and for the girl to leave it with her...

She switches her phone off, her dark eyes staring into nothingness, tears slowly filling them. Then she sits down at the little counter, hesitates, switches her phone back on, turns to 'Contacts' and slowly taps Ron's name. Anna lifts the phone in a shaking hand, biting her lips, giving her eyes a quick swipe. "Come on, Ron," she mutters at the second ring, pulling a face, knowing that he will need longer than that to even get his phone out!

"Anna, how are you?"

The calm voice somehow helps Anna to release the breath she had been holding, and she gasps, "Oh Ron, she has disappeared. I mean, the girl from the resort rang that she didn't show at breakfast time and no one has seen her this morning. She is not in her room; they looked around the resort... Do you think the men found her?"

"Slow down a moment and paddle back a bit." Ron's voice has changed, and Anna finds his cool, slower-than-usual words calming. "I presume you're talking about Martha?"

Anna confirms this and repeats that Martha can't be found in the resort.

"Do you know which apartment she's staying at, and can I just walk in?"

Anna describes how to find the apartment on the corner. "The only security is the lock on the door... but I don't have a key – how will we convince the reception staff to let us in?"

"I'll go and have a look," Ron says, and then chuckles. "I do have some special skills when it comes to door locks..."

Anna feels it is probably best not to ask. She can tell from the way Ron talks and sounds that he is moving already and although this should make her feel better, instead, it makes fear come into her heart in large, steady waves. The fact that he is going to check it out instantly can only mean that he takes it *very* seriously! She thanks him and rings off.

Anna looks round the tiny shop for a moment, then gets busy. Within fifteen minutes the shop is ready to be locked up, and she leaves, her hands shaking. She sends a text to Ron to let him know that she's on her way, ETA twenty minutes or thereabouts.

Martha's apartment looks immaculate as ever, apart from Ron's presence. Anna tries to smile a greeting, but the tears are too close for comfort, so she gives up. Ron just looks up from reading one of Martha's notebooks and nods.

"Hi, Anna, thanks for coming over. I'm just looking through her notebooks to see if she has written anything down that will explain things."

Anna nods, and looks round, commenting that nothing seems to be out of place.

"Martha's bag has gone," Ron says, his own steady gaze trailing round the studio apartment.

Anna moves closer to the little table, then gives a cry as she spots the small, stout notebook near Ron's elbow. "Martha's Lifeline!" she gasps, half sobbing, as just seeing the notebook gives her a real shock.

Ron has opened the notebook already, remembering his conversation with Martha on the day she brought him coffee. His lopsided grin appears when he spots the references to himself whilst flicking through the pages – but that grin is nowhere to be seen when he gets to the last page. Anna claps both hands over her mouth when she sees Ron turning a little pale and grave. He looks up and hesitates a moment before turning the page towards her. In Martha's handwriting it just says, "Seen socks, sandals and goatie. Going towards harbour. Need to tell R."

For a moment they look at one another, and Anna staggers towards the bed, sits down and just cries. It is clear that the men found Martha before she had a chance to tell Ron. She could be anywhere, and not necessarily in the land of the living either. Ron doesn't say anything, doesn't tell her to cheer up, doesn't move at all, in fact. When Anna finally stops crying, he simply digs a packet of tissues out of his pockets and hands her one, still without saying anything.

Anna wipes her face, blows her nose, then looks at him, trying to sound ready for action. "What now? Where do we start?"

He looks at her in surprise. "You're not looking anywhere," he says, then smiles a little as if that will change anything. "My mates will be here soon enough, and we'll look."

Anna frowns and shakes her head. Ron's eyes narrow a little, and she just knows he's going to sigh at her stubbornness, and she even knows how his voice will sound when he will try to explain to her how nice it is that she's offering to help but that this is going to be a job for the experts and all that... Before he even has a chance, she says firmly, "I'm in on this. I can sail a boat to wherever you need to go, I can speak Greek, I know the people and – well, I'm in on this. Martha is my friend." She clenches her fists, for she almost said, "Martha *was* my friend."

Ron purses his lips, and Anna waits for the sigh, but to her surprise he just nods. "As long as you stay close to us. These guys are dangerous."

Anna is more than happy to promise to do that, fear for Martha's safety churning inside her.

Ron steps outside onto the balcony, speaking into his phone. Anna is left behind, wondering how the men managed to take Martha, and where from. Would she have walked towards the harbour? Not likely, as she had seen 'goatie' going that way. Martha would have stayed clear. Anna tries to picture Martha's morning, then steps outside as well, her eyes travelling round the resort, from Martha's studio towards the dining room, where Martha must have been headed for breakfast when the men found her.

Anna follows the path slowly, just praying that she will find something, anything... She can feel the dark feeling of hopelessness crowding in, whispering to give it up, to leave it to the professionals, and that it's too late anyway, why would Martha even be alive? But she carries on, praying, trusting, hoping...

She comes to a corner, and the dry ground under the bushes looks different. Anna holds her breath, wondering whether she is making things up just because she is so desperate or whether the earth around the bushes is really scratched and changed. She looks back and gives a little shriek, as Ron is just behind her, his eyes intense. He nods when she points out the disturbed sand, and both look around the bush.

Anna's heart is beating fast; part of her is terrified at the thought of finding Martha behind or under the bush, dead. It has definitely been battered and suffered from the hands of someone devoid of green thumbs.

Then, suddenly, Ron and Anna both exclaim and point at the same time. In the sand is a large letter D, with one corner slightly scuffed out.

Anna looks up. "Dia! It must be, mustn't it? Let's go," she says, turning. Fingers screw around her upper arm instantly, stopping her in her tracks.

"No. Not now, not yet. We must wait for dark."

Anna's mouth drops. *Ron wants to wait the entire day whilst Martha is in danger, kidnapped, kept dead or alive on the island? Seriously?*

Ron's face tightens when he sees the shock and outrage on her face. Then he asks quietly, "What do you think will happen to Martha when they see us sailing up to the island?"

Anna sucks in air, her dark eyes widening in horror.

Ron nods, satisfied that his point has been made. "Yes, exactly. We have to wait, however hard that is. It's the only way. Now, go home, sort out the boat, and come to the little harbour as soon as it's dark. We will meet you there; bring Dimitris if you need to," he smiles, clearly trying to make her think everything will be alright. After all, he and his friends have it all in hand.

Anna knows though. She knows that the tiny area of scratched earth under the bush could easily have been missed. She knows it will take more than clever, strong men to bring this horrible incident to a positive outcome. The question is, what *is* a positive outcome, and will they all look at the outcome as being positive? Anna swallows, trying to pray. "Thy will be done..." She tries to mean it, then nods at Ron and leaves the resort, fear and hope fighting each other, leaving her breathless.

30

MARTHA CAN FEEL HERSELF RESURFACING, HER stomach protesting as well as feeling very empty. Her first thought is about how cold she is and how hard the ground feels under her back. She also thinks how very, very scared she is. For a few seconds she allows her mind to give in to her terror, feeling its waves crashing over her head, filling up all her senses, like a storm that suddenly lands on a lake. Then she senses another voice, a voice commanding the waves to be still and for peace to reign. Martha holds her breath, stunned to realise that the waves of fear will obey this voice, and she can hear the Slavic accent of Pastor Volodya urging her to fear not, only to trust. Martha wants to, she really does, but surely her fear is too great? *I can do all things,* she tells her mind, expecting it to mock her, to laugh its raucous laugh, but her mind does grow quiet – quieter than Martha imagined it ever would. In this quiet she can hear the men's voices just outside wherever she is. Martha doesn't dare to open her eyes; the nausea is sure to become full-blown sickness once she allows daylight to peek in.

In a bid to ignore her stomach's antics, Martha focusses on the voices, knowing one will belong to 'Goatie' and one to the younger man that was waiting for her behind the bushes. When the third voice pipes up,

Martha's heart stops and she can feel herself going completely still; then her heart starts up again, doing double time as if to make up for the lack of action earlier. *What is he doing here? Why...* Her mind races off in various directions, and she can feel the shakes settling in with a vengeance. *This can't be true! Why would he even...* No still small voice is heard now, and Martha finds the tidal wave of terror crashing upon her heart's shores. *Not him, Lord, please not him, I can't do this, I'm too...* Martha stops herself then, although the effort is almost more than she can cope with. Yes, she is far too weak to deal with him, far too fragile to face him, far too petrified to see him... 'Goatie' and the diver were bad enough, and somehow Martha found a tiny part of herself thinking she could escape them again through her ingenuity and determination. After all, she had escaped them before, hadn't she? She had been absolutely determined, and with a lot of effort managed to cut the ropes and hide in the cave. This, though... this man is a different matter altogether, and Martha can feel all her clever plans and dreams draining away, leaving a dark, black, gaping hole where determination and will-power were so prominent just a few moments ago.

Where am I anyway? She is pretty sure she heard one of the men mention Dia when they ambushed her. When she managed to get free for a brief moment, she screamed as she fell into a bush and just had time to scribble a 'D' on the ground – but then she was pulled back and her mouth covered to silence her. *I doubt anyone will find the D – and even if they do, it won't mean anything... But if this is Dia, perhaps some of the day visitors might find me...?*

"She'll be fine there, and we can sort her out later," the posh voice says, shattering Martha's momentary thoughts of hope and causing her to take gasping breaths with each word she hears. "What is important is this latest shipment though. I'm not sure about the quality of that larger amphora," the voice continues, sounding a little whiny like a spoilt child, and Martha hears 'Goatie's' voice explaining the trouble they had with the larger amphorae in the area.

The voices move away from where Martha lies down, and when she can no longer hear them, she carefully opens her eyes. Immediately, her head spins and spins, along with her stomach, but after a few cautious tries everything stays in its place, including her stomach content.

As Martha looks round, her mind is already thinking of ways to escape. Of course, her handbag is nowhere to be found. She sighs, trying to think whether she has anything in her pockets – but no, her shorts were clean on that morning and she hadn't put anything in. Not that she carries knives or scissors in her pockets as a rule, but somehow she needs to check everything methodically. Either that or lose her mind in blind panic.

"I need to get out, preferably now," she mutters to herself, driven by the sense of urgency and doom, knowing that the posh voice will return and 'sort her out'. "He tried to sort me out before, and there is no helpful sister nearby this time to save my life." She can feel his hands round her throat and actually finds herself struggling to breathe. "Stop, and calm down," she tells herself sternly, even though her voice is quavering.

Martha tries to wriggle her hands, but the rope around her wrist is stiff and well-knotted. She gives up after a while and tries to see her ankles. They are just as well tied-up, it seems, and Martha has to give up; annoyed, as she is sure it should be possible to get out – to get her hands to the front, then work the knot on her ankles, or at least to sit up and move around the cave, or maybe even get out of the cave. Instead, she can't move at all, her hands behind her; everything is uncomfortable and hard. She is no longer cold; only around her heart it feels the cold has permanently lodged itself. She lies down quietly, spent, worried... debating with herself what to do now.

Looking at the rocky ceiling above her head, Martha suddenly realises that she hasn't actually been sick. In fact, her stomach has calmed down, apart from feeling empty. She ponders this and smiles a tiny, shaken smile to herself. "Fear not, I can do all things, my strength is made perfect in weakness," she whispers, wondering if it really can be true, and if she will be able to hold on to all those promises when the men return.

It is evening before they come, finding Martha asleep from sheer exhaustion and suspense! She wakes up with a muffled shriek when 'Diver' nudges her with his foot, then drags her into a sitting position, offering her some water. Martha hesitates a moment, visons of spiked water, or poison even, racing around her head. Then her thirst wins out and she drinks greedily from the lukewarm water. She looks at the man's hard face, wondering if she should ask him what they are planning to do with her. Then she decides that she doesn't particularly want to know... Also, she fears that if she speaks up, her ex-husband will come into the cave. She is definitely not ready for a confrontation with him. The idea of seeing him face-to-face again makes her whole body shake. The diver obviously notices, as he looks at her, sneering, opening his mouth as if to say something, then changes his mind. He puts the top back on the bottle and walks out of the cave, leaving Martha in the semi-darkness.

She shuffles back on her bottom until she hits the back of the cave, glad to sit up for a bit. Her back and legs ache, and all over, her body feels stiff. "I'm obviously not cut out for camping," she mumbles to herself, trying to keep the darkness out of her mind. She makes herself smaller when she hears the men arguing, and she can tell from William's voice that he is about to explode. "They must have said no to him," she groans, rolling her eyes, then stops in surprise. "Normally I would be a crying, shaking mess if he talked like that, and although I'm scared, I'm sort of... alright?"

Martha thinks about this for a while, and in the end, she finds herself humming an old hymn. "When peace like a river attendeth my soul; when sorrows like sea billows roll... Yes," she sighs suddenly, "yes, that is it, and I had forgotten all those years. It's not about now and here and others, it's about my soul and eternity and having a Saviour!" Tears come then, warm healing tears, cleansing her, restoring her, leaving her drained but full.

When she is calm again, she wipes her face dry on her shoulder, her arms sore from being in the same position for so long! The voices have stopped, and Martha tries to listen hard. After a very long time of rustling, shuffling and other odd noises, it goes quiet. Too quiet almost, and Martha shivers. *Have the men gone, leaving me here in the dark, by myself, for good? Nobody will ever find me, at least not before it's too late,* she worries, all her peace dissolving into the darkness. *And then...* She stops, then, slowly forces words past her lips: "I... WILL... NOT... FEAR." She breathes in, and in, and in, then out, out and out – until she feels that calm has been restored.

When the whooshing and hissing sounds in her ears have stopped, she can hear another noise, one that she recognises at once. William is snoring, and Martha, for one vindictive moment, wishes she were free, free to sit on top of him with her hands round his throat for a change. Then she blushes – what a thought! She frowns at herself; after all, that would put her at the same level as him! Still, the idea that he is going free annoys her. This makes her wonder why he is here in the first place. Hardly his scene!

Suddenly Martha remembers the large amphora that William gave her when they were dating. She loved its warm colours and felt it was such a clear sign of his great love for her – such a valuable and beautiful gift. It disappeared shortly after she married William and he said that their house had been broken into. "We are so lucky that nothing else was taken," he reassured her.

Is William involved with these thieves? Is that where my amphora came from? And was it really stolen or was that another lie? Somehow Martha isn't surprised at all. William's conscience is obviously not working very well, and his love of all things expensive is stamped all over his life. "Oh dear..." she sighs, praying and wondering about the future – *well, the future as in the next few hours, at least...* She's too sore and stiff to lie down again, and somehow, sitting up makes it all feel more bearable, even though she is cold. Martha decides to hum herself warm, trying to think of all the songs and hymns that she can remember. In the middle of Luther's hymn, she stops, sure that she heard something just outside the cave. *Have the other men returned? Did William wake up?* She can still hear the snoring, but Martha stays very quiet, listening intently.

31

ANNA GASPS AS SIX MEN APPEAR SUDDENLY OUT
of the dark near the harbour wall, just where their boat is
tied up. Dimitris sucks in air as well, wishing that he were
at home, wishing he had never... but then, Martha was in
danger, and it was his duty to do what was right at all
times, never mind the cost or his fears.

Dimitris and Anna watch the men make their way to
the boat with quick, confident steps. One of the tall men
steps ahead a little bit, and Anna feels strangely relieved
to recognise Ron's cool voice when he calls out softly. He
steps aboard and shakes hands with Dimitris. He nods
and grins his lopsided grin at Anna, looking even more
odd as his face has been blackened with camouflage paint.
Anna bites her lips. *I'm glad I'm on the same side as these
guys!*

"These are my friends," Ron explains, making a
sweeping gesture with one hand, and all five men nod or
salute Dimitris and Anna. Anna tries to smile at them all,
feeling intimidated and nervous. The men seem very calm
and their movements show that they all know what to do.
Ron turns back to Dimitris. "Could you drop us off
somewhere quite close to Dia, preferably somewhere
where the men are not likely to see you?"

Dimitris nods, and pulls out a local map that he uses for tourists. He points at the side of the island. "This area has lots of little coves and inlets but can be quite rough. No larger boat would ever approach the island from here."

Ron looks at the map, together with another man. They call the others over and in quiet voices discuss their plans. It is clear that Ron is in charge, and his quiet voice just sounds like soft, calm murmurings. Anna looks at the group of tall, broad-shouldered men, their confidence covering them as the camo does their faces. She has to admire their strength and calmness, but at the same time she wonders if it will be enough. Will their strength be enough to find and rescue Martha? Will their plans be sufficient; will their training be the right kind of preparation?

"If you drop us off *here*" – Ron points and Dimitris nods – "then we'll use our little boat to get ashore *here*." Ron pokes the map again and the other men look closely at it, tracing its outlines with their fingers.

Dimitris points at the map, and sounding only a tiny bit nervous, suggests that Martha is probably held in some caves just *there*, with a path reaching it just *here*...

Ron looks serious, and he and the men start discussing ways and means, priorities and plans.

Anna turns away from the little group, tears filling her eyes. *Will Martha really be in the caves? Dimitris thinks she must be, for it's really the best place to hide. What if the men have killed her though? After all, she could be lying on the sea floor, amidst the amphorae. Even these men, in spite of their obvious confidence, can't perform miracles, and a whole day has passed since Martha disappeared. She must be so scared as well.*

Soon the boat is pushed off and glides out of the little harbour. Anna sits still in a corner, feeling queasy, not from the gentle rocking boat but through fears and worry. She knows that she should pray, and trust and show faith, but thoughts of Martha in danger consume her mind. Snippets of Pastor Volodya's sermon float in and out of her head, but Anna struggles to do what she knows is right. After all, Martha has been through so much already; first her husband, leaving her with such mental scars, and now this! She nearly shrieks when a dark figure kneels down next to her.

It's Ron, his eyes serious, a small white line around them where he didn't put any camo. "You're worried about Martha," he states. "I promise we'll do what we can, Anna."

She nods, wipes a rather obvious tear away, and then asks whether he thinks Martha is still alive.

Ron nods. "Yes, I'm reasonably confident about that. The men wouldn't have taken her with them if they planned to kill her," he says.

"What if they wanted to buy just a bit of time? What if they killed her and just dropped her into the sea?" Anna doesn't bother drying her tears now. The fact that Ron stays silent doesn't make it any better. She knows that she is right, but she hoped Ron would deny it and prove her wrong. The fact that he doesn't makes her feel almost sick with grief, even though she knows that there is hope. Ron is right; after all, the men might have just hidden her on Dia, and Martha might be perfectly alright!

The trip to Dia seems endless, and Anna feels relieved when the dark mass shows up. When Dimitris cuts the engines, Ron touches her shoulder lightly before getting up and walking over to him.

One last look at the map, one last whispered conversation, and the men walk to the back of the boat, launching what looks like a large inflatable dingy. They climb in swiftly, six tall men with rucksacks and painted faces, black gloves and bulging pockets. Anna hardly registers them leaving the boat. Then Dimitris plops down beside her. "Well, let's hope they can find Martha soon!" he whispers to her. Anna just nods.

It is very quiet in the night, not a sound can be heard apart from the soft splashing made by the waves hitting their boat. Anna looks out but can't see or hear the men in their little boat. *Will they manage to land on one of the little rough beaches?*

Martha sits as still as she can, hardly daring to breathe. She's sure she heard something besides William's snoring. She strains her eyes looking to where she knows the dark entrance is. She swallows down a whimper when she's sure that an even darker shape has just appeared in the entrance! A soft voice suddenly whispers, "Martha?" Martha can't stop the gasp that jumps out of her throat before holding her breath again. A torch flashes on instantly, half blinding her, and she finds it impossible to stop the whimpers coming out of her mouth. The light is dimmed a little, and a large figure looms up right next to her.

"Shh, it's just me, Martha. It's Ron." The cool voice somehow makes it through to her, and Martha goes quiet again, relief filling her eyes with tears. She sniffles a bit to try to control them before they spill out, steaming up her glasses.

"Let me just cut these ropes," he continues, after gloved hands feel her wrists.

Martha tries to stay still as Ron hacks away at her ropes, thinking how much quicker this is done in movies, worried about William next door. Finally, her hands are free, and tears come after all when circulation is fully restored to them.

Ron rubs her wrists and her hands to help, and Martha does her best to control her sobs. He produces a tissue and she wipes her nose with shaking hands whilst he chops away at the rope round her ankles. Soon she is free, but unable to move, stiff from the day on the hard ground.

Another dark shape appears and Martha half shrieks, worried that it's William! It turns out to be one of Ron's friends though, who briefly nods at her before whispering to Ron in quick, short sentences.

Ron turns to Martha. "Do you know who the guy next door is?" he asks, and Martha nods vigorously. She explains that his name is William Penworth-Taylor, her ex-husband, who is somehow connected to the thieves! She has to giggle when the two large men with their camo faces stare at her in shock. She nods and explains that she only found out today that he was here, and she tells them that the other two seemed to have gone off, probably on another raid, she suspects. The men nod, and Ron and the other man whisper quickly before the man disappears into the dark again.

Ron turns to Martha again and says softly, "I'll have to switch off the torch for a bit, as we want to catch the men on their way back. Even a small torch can be seen for miles, and I don't want them to be alerted."

Martha nods, but in the dark it's a lot harder to stay composed and tear-free...

Time crawls by, and Martha tries to focus on restoring some feeling to her hands and feet to make the time pass quicker. Suddenly she hears quiet men's voices, and she grabs Ron's arm in the dark. Straightaway, a gloved hand covers her mouth lightly and he breathes in her ear. "No move."

Martha nods in the dark, and stays as still as she can, listening hard.

Ron has put one hand on her shoulder, and she can feel his quiet tension, ready to jump into action at a moment's notice. Suddenly there are a lot of noises, scuffles, grunts and then an angry voice calling out, "What do you think you're..." Martha only realises that she's been squeezing Ron's arm in excitement when he prises her fingers a little looser...

After a while the noises stop, apart from William's posh voice, sounding outraged, demanding an answer, an explanation, better treatment, a proper seat... Martha rolls her eyes; *some things obviously never change!*

Footsteps sound; then light from a powerful torch floods their cave and Martha shields her eyes. Ron stands up and his friend explains that they got the two guys, as well as "sleepyhead" from the cave next door.

Ron helps Martha up and holds on tightly to her arm as she tries to find her balance, groaning softly over her stiff legs and back. "Let's go and have a look at your ex, shall we?" He grins at her, and she shudders, hating the idea, even though William will be unable to harm her now!

They leave the cave where she has spent her long, miserable day, and just outside the next-door cave she finds more camo-faced men. They grin at her and point to the cave opening, welcoming them through. Martha hesitates; she really has no desire to see William face-to-face, nor the other two men, for that matter! Ron grins his unique smile at her and leaves her with one of his friends just outside the opening. He goes in, and Martha shivers when she hears his cool voice talking to the three rogues. She can't hear what he says, but she just finds herself glad to be on the right side of that voice! Somehow, she can imagine how scary he must be as an enemy. *Imagine waking up with his large figure looming over you, face all painted black. Add that to the controlled voice...* Martha is glad she decided to stay out here!

Ron soon comes back, smiling at her. "Let's go," he says. "We'll get you back to the boat, Martha, and then we'll sort out a way to pick these guys up."

Martha nods, and follows Ron and two of the men to their little rubber dingy, forcing herself to let them help her in carefully. The men paddle swiftly away from the rocky shore, and soon Martha can make out the dark outline of a larger boat. *Anna's boat!*

Finally, they reach it, the rubber dingy softly bumping against the colourful side of the much larger vessel. Anna's and Dimitris' faces appear, anxiously peering into the dark at the approaching little craft.

Ron calls out, "We're here. Martha is here. She's fine!"

Anna shrieks and does a wild dance, laughing and crying at the same time, leaving Dimitris grinning and rolling his eyes, jokingly apologising for his wild sister... Ron and Dimitris help Martha aboard the boat, and Anna embraces her, both women crying and hugging.

Ron briefly explains what happened on Dia. "We found the caves alright – bit tricky in the dark! Fortunately, there was a tiny nightlight in the cave, so we found the entrance quicker than we expected. Also, the guy could snore for England," he laughs, "so all we had to do was follow the sound. Once we were in the caves, we split up when we realised there were several rooms. I found Martha, and my friends went to wake Mr Sleepyhead."

Dimitris laughs.

"Then all we needed to do was wait for his mates, because Martha told us that the other two had gone out. So we prepared a nice welcome for them..."

"I bet the men were surprised, thinking they had come back to their hideout for some sleep!"

Ron grins, and explains that they were caught red-handed as well, as they found several amphorae, most still wet, clearly from the sea bottom!

"What do you want to do now?" Dimitris asks, and Ron explains that the men will need to be taken off the island. Dimitris shows on his map where he can land the boat, and Ron agrees. Ron asks Dimitris to take them there so they can pick up his friends and the three criminals to take them to the authorities.

32

WHILST DIMITRIS STARTS THE BOAT, ANNA AND Martha find a hiding spot, as Martha is determined to avoid William. Anna isn't too keen to meet the thieves either, so they huddle in a corner, whispering.

Ron watches them go and grins a little. He stands near Dimitris and tells him where his sister and Martha have gone, when he sees him looking around concerned.

"The cove is just round this corner," Dimitris points out, steering the boat without effort it seems, in spite of the darkness. Soon the little landing area looms up, and he slows the boat down.

Ron and his friends get ready to disembark, and the two women and Dimitris watch them climb overboard onto the little landing area. Then the three men disappear into the darkness – and the waiting begins.

Martha feels herself shivering, part of her worried that in the time it took them to get here, the three thieves will have escaped somehow, ready to now take their revenge.

Soon they can hear voices, one especially, an angry, posh-sounding voice droning on and on and on... Martha rolls her eyes, and sighs to Anna, "My ex-husband... He will be so angry right now. Even the slightest change to his plans used to send him over the cliff, so imagine his fury now!"

Anna giggles, and the two listen to the voices getting closer. Soon the camo-faced men help the three prisoners onto the boat. They steer the men into a corner out of the way.

"I just don't want to see William," Martha whispers, her heart doing overtime as it is, listening to the belligerent voice demanding and accusing constantly.

Anna agrees; it doesn't sound like a good idea to say hello to William just now… She wonders if he was like this when they were married, and when she asks, Martha nods.

"Yes – and I accepted it, as he always made it sound so reasonable and managed to put the blame on me. It made me feel guilty for even thinking badly of him, and I felt I should have tried harder to please him. Only occasionally did I feel that, surely, he had a part to play in it as well – but he would really go off one if I hinted at his responsibility or the fact that his reaction wasn't the correct one. After a few times, I gave up and just took the path of least resistance. I just wrapped myself in a long coat of self-pity and let all the storms pass over me, rather than do what was right."

At least the boat's engine drowns out most of the words, as well as other noises, and both women gasp when a dark figure suddenly appears in front of them. It's Ron, who just grins and apologises, even though he doesn't sound too sorry… Anna asks what they will do with the three thieves, and Ron explains that they have already warned the authorities, who will be waiting for them when they get to the harbour. He says, "I'm glad we managed to get all three, and the best part was that you were alright, Martha." He smiles at her and she blushes.

Then her smile freezes on her lips as she hears William's voice demanding that Martha speaks to him. His furious voice lists all the things he will do to her when his hands are free.

Ron sees her face change and something in him stirs. He knows it won't be a good idea for him to go and see William just now and he is surprised by the intensity of his anger. Seeing her hands shake in the semi-darkness doesn't improve matters at all. He gets up, trying to make it look smooth and controlled, and excuses himself for a moment. "I'll be right back," he says, and walks with confident steps to one of his friends. He whispers some instructions to him, making sure it's not sounding too vindictive, and his friend just laughs. "Just sort the guy out; tell him we'll pop something in his mouth if he doesn't switch the noise off," he says grimly, part of him hoping that William *will* continue... He turns back to the women straight away, and the friend walks over to where the thieves are being kept. Within seconds William's voice has stopped, and Ron feels very pleased with the quick result, grinning and lifting his chin at his friend when he comes back in view.

Martha wondered how they managed to make William stay quiet. She looks at Ron. Should she ask him? There is something hard in his eyes though, and somehow, she feels it's probably better that she doesn't ask...

The harbour shows up in the dark, the night sky looking eerie with the flashing lights from waiting police cars. William's voice is heard again, but he stops mid-sentence when several of the camo-faced men turn round and look as if they're ready to move towards him. Martha is amazed, and she looks at Anna, who looks just as impressed. The two women look at Ron, who just smiles and shrugs. "He obviously ran out of words," he jokes, not prepared to share his instructions.

Martha giggles. "Well, that's a first, then! I'm glad he stopped though. I just find it really hard to listen to his voice. It… it brings back bad memories and makes me feel guilty that I lived with it for so long. I feel so foolish that I believed him and just allowed it all to happen!"

Anna squeezes her hand, pointing out that we can all make mistakes and that relationships can be so complex!

When they arrive at the harbour, the police board the little boat, and soon the three men are taken away. Ron returns and asks Martha if she wants to tell the police about her kidnapping and press charges, or whether she wants to stay out of the picture completely.

"I'd rather stay out of it," Martha says, wondering if that is again taking the easy way out. "I just don't want to see them or speak to them. I'd rather just forget the whole thing and enjoy my time as holiday rep."

Ron nods, and disappears again. He comes back after talking to one of the officers, who all look like aliens with the flashing lights against the black sky. He talks to Dimitris, and then comes to say goodbye to the women.

"My friends John and Lou will walk you back to the resort, Martha," he says, and she nods, even though the idea of having to walk along the quiet road with two unknown big men is almost scarier than walking the familiar road by herself! He must have guessed her thoughts again, and smiles at her. "It's just to make sure. You've had a bad day and a long night, so just allow them to get you back safely."

Martha gives in, as graciously as she can, and even manages to thank him.

"Then tomorrow evening... would you two ladies like to go for a meal at the resort?" He grins his lopsided grin, and Anna accepts straight away.

Martha feels the heat rolling into her face like the waves on the sand just behind her. The feeling in her stomach is unusual as well, and she finds herself accepting with a rather goofy smile, surprising herself – so confused by her own feelings that she doesn't notice Ron's gleaming eyes and his quick wink to Anna. He looks very pleased with himself, though, when he gets off the boat, whistling out of tune whilst walking up to the waiting police cars.

Martha rests that day, then resumes her job the following morning. She shudders when she thinks back to the conversation with the manager. He wasn't impressed that she had been involved with kidnappers, thieves and smugglers, no matter how unwillingly! "What were you thinking, woman?" Even though the day hadn't been going that long, alcohol wafted across to Martha already, not helping her to stay calm and composed at all. Her shaking hands almost destroyed the locket, and for one brief moment she felt grateful that the chain was such good quality, as anything less would have snapped by now! In the end the manager grunted something that sounded very much like, "Make sure it's the last time," which of course Martha was only too happy to promise! She heard some people discussing the haul, but she managed to steer away from the conversation, although part of her worried that William would be let out on bail and then would make a beeline for the resort!

Later, in the afternoon, she stands on her balcony, looking at the beautiful sapphire water, wondering if she should go to her little beach. She sighs. "I'm still too tired, and part of me is afraid of leaving the resort as well. I just hope that this fear will go." Martha pulls a face, knowing very well that in order for the fear to go, she will have to overcome it! This time she refuses to slither down into the victim mindset. On the other hand, having to face and confront her fear makes her feel exhausted already. Instead she gets her paper and pencils out, and staring off into the sunny distance, she thinks back over the last few days. She remembers the cave with its hard ground, the ropes keeping her tied up, immobile. She remembers the feeling of peace and how her heart was free even though she wasn't able to free herself. She smiles a little, picturing herself, a thin, shivering mess in a dark cave, her ex-husband snoring away next door, but her heart had been strangely warmed, and peace had attended her soul like a river. She pulls a face at those fragments of words and hymns, glad that Ron isn't here to guess her thoughts. Soon the brown and grey pencils move across the paper with quick, confident strokes, her hands skilled and purposeful. The cave takes shape, it's darkness and hardness well pictured. Lighter colours depict her bonds, shredded in the middle of the cave, and an even lighter, huddled shape is placed near the back wall, hands raised in gratefulness and praise.

It is almost time for dinner by the time Martha puts her pencils down. She feels exhausted, thrilled, broken, healed – and just refreshed. She leans back in her chair, looking at the paper in front of her, slightly blurred because of her tear-filled eyes. She sniffs, feeling free and even happy. That is, until she realises the time!

Instant shakes set in. She's having dinner with Ron – and Anna, of course, but what will she say all through dinner to Ron? What if he insists that she eats and drinks certain things? What if he drinks way too much and gets aggressive? What if...

"No fear. I will not fear," she says out loud, making herself jump. She takes a deep breath, then stands up, and with determined movements tidies up her pencils, putting the paper away safely, and tidies herself up ready for dinner. Yes, she is scared, worried about all the 'what ifs' – but she has to accept that her heart is fluttering with more excitement than fear. For instead of fear, or at least caution, her heart just wants to sing, making her move faster than usual – and if she didn't know better, she would think that she was actually looking forward to this dinner!

Martha struggles to slow herself down on her way to the dining room, and groans at herself when she hears her way too exuberant voice greeting Ron who is waiting for her and Anna at the entrance. It's only Anna's pleased smile and kind eyes that stop Martha from telling herself off. There is no place in her heart for fear, and maybe that is what she fears the most just now!